My Trees in the Himalayas

Ruskin Bond has been writing for over sixty years, and now has over 120 titles in print—novels, collections of short stories, poetry, essays, anthologies and books for children. His first novel, *The Room on the Roof*, received the prestigious John Llewellyn Rhys Prize in 1957. He has also received the Padma Shri (1999), the Padma Bhushan (2014) and two awards from Sahitya Akademi—one for his short stories and another for his writings for children. In 2012, the Delhi government gave him its Lifetime Achievement Award.

Born in 1934, Ruskin Bond grew up in Jamnagar, Shimla, New Delhi and Dehradun. Apart from three years in the UK, he has spent all his life in India, and now lives in Mussoorie with his adopted family.

My Trees in the Himalayas

Selected and Compiled by
RUSKIN BOND

Published by
Rupa Publications India Pvt. Ltd 2018
7/16, Ansari Road, Daryaganj
New Delhi 110002

Sales centres:
Allahabad Bengaluru Chennai
Hyderabad Jaipur Kathmandu
Kolkata Mumbai

Copyright © Ruskin Bond 2018

This is a work of fiction. Names, characters, places and incidents are either the product of the author's imagination or are used fictitiously and any resemblance to any actual person, living or dead, events or locales is entirely coincidental.

All rights reserved.
No part of this publication may be reproduced, transmitted, or stored in a retrieval system, in any form or by any means, electronic, mechanical, photocopying, recording or otherwise, without the prior permission of the publisher.

ISBN: 978-81-936-6952-5

Sixth impression 2022

10 9 8 7 6

Printed in India

This book is sold subject to the condition that it shall not, by way of trade or otherwise, be lent, resold, hired out, or otherwise circulated, without the publisher's prior consent, in any form of binding or cover other than that in which it is published.

CONTENTS

Introduction	vii
The Nightingale and the Rose Oscar Wilde	1
My Trees in the Himalayas Ruskin Bond	9
The Gift of the Magi O. Henry	13
The Folder Noel Langley	20
What Happened to a Father Who Became a Schoolboy F. Anstey	30
The Beggar Anton Chekhov	48
Reading and Books in the Valley Upendra Arora	55

The Little Ghost	64
Hugh Walpole	
The Tale of a Child	82
Josef Bard	
Dusk	105
'Saki' (H.H. Munro)	
Boy Among the Writers	111
David Garnett	
The Last Lesson	123
Alphonse Daudet	

INTRODUCTION

I have a window. My armchair has been strategically placed right in front of it, because I do not wish to miss out on any of the happenings in the great outdoors. Those who advertise rooms or flats to let often describe them as 'Room with bath' or 'Room with tea and coffee-making facilities'. A more attractive proposition would be 'Room with window', for without a view a room is hardly a living place—merely a place of transit. My bedroom window opens on to blue skies, mountains striding away into the far distance, winding rivers in the valley below, and, just to bring me down to earth, the local television tower.

On the window's left is the walnut tree, the source of an annual basket of walnuts. A grove of pine trees on the hillside next to my cottage is also visible—I go there often to sit under those trees and listen to the soft swishing sounds of the wind.

I walk among the trees outside my window often, acknowledging their presence with a touch of my hand against their trunks. The oak has been there the longest, and the wind has bent its upper branches and twisted a few so that it looks shaggy and undistinguished. But it is a good tree for the privacy of birds. Sometimes it seems completely uninhabited until there is a whining sound, as of a helicopter approaching, and a party of long-tailed blue magpies flies across the forest glade.

There is another favourite pastime I indulge in quite often. That is reading short stories and imagining them being played out in my garden. On numerous occasions, I have sat here and tried to picture how Della and Jim from O. Henry's *The Gift of Magi* would look when they saw each other's Christmas gifts, have spent hours in daydreaming about the nightingale, from Oscar Wilde's *The Nightingale and the Rose*, singing in my garden. I think about how the child's ghost would be in person, from Hugh Walpole's *The Little Ghost*. I have imagined David Garnett meeting all the famous writers he has mentioned in *Boy Among the Writers*, and also the little classroom in nineteenth-century Alsace from Alphonse Daudet's *The Last Lesson*.

I have compiled in this collection these and a few more short stories that will make you daydream as well—about gardens and trees and the simple joys of life. So, lose yourself in them and picture a world away from the mundane...

Ruskin Bond

THE NIGHTINGALE AND THE ROSE

Oscar Wilde

'She said that she would dance with me if I brought her red roses,' cried the young Student, 'but in all my garden there is no red rose.'

From her nest in the holm-oak tree the Nightingale heard him, and she looked out through the leaves and wondered.

'No red rose in all my garden!' he cried, and his beautiful eyes filled with tears. 'Ah, on what little things does happiness depend! I have read all that the wise men have written, and all the secrets of philosophy are mine, yet for want of a red rose is my life made wretched.'

'Here at last is a true lover,' said the Nightingale. 'Night after night have I sung of him, though I knew him not: night after night have I told his story to the stars and now I see him. His hair is dark as the hyacinth-blossom, and his lips are red as the rose of his desire; but passion has made his face like pale ivory, and sorrow has set her seal upon his brow.'

'The Prince gives a ball tomorrow night,' murmured the

young Student, 'and my love will be of the company. If I bring her a red rose she will dance with me till dawn. If I bring her a red rose, I shall hold her in my arms, and she will lean her head upon my shoulder, and her hand will be clasped in mine. But there is no red rose in my garden, so I shall sit lonely, and she will pass me by. She will have no heed of me, and my heart will break.'

'Here, indeed, is the true lover,' said the Nightingale. 'What I sing of, he suffers: what is joy to me, to him is pain. Surely, love is a wonderful thing. It is more precious than emeralds, and dearer than fine opals. Pearls and pomegranates cannot buy it, nor is it set forth in the market-place. It may not be purchased of the merchants, nor can it be weighed out in the balance for gold.'

'The musicians will sit in their gallery,' said the young Student, 'and play upon their stringed instruments, and my love will dance to the sound of the harp and the violin. She will dance so lightly that her feet will not touch the floor, and the courtiers in their gay dresses will throng round her. But with me she will not dance, for I have no red rose to give her'; and he flung himself down on the grass, and buried his face in his hands and wept.

'Why is he weeping?' asked a little Green Lizard, as he ran past him with his tail in the air.

'Why, indeed?' said a Butterfly, who was fluttering about after it sunbeam.

'Why, indeed?' whispered it Daisy to his neighbour, in a soft, low voice.

'He is weeping for a red rose,' said the Nightingale.

'For a red rose?' they cried; 'how very ridiculous!' and the little Lizard, who was something of a cynic, laughed outright.

But the Nightingale understood the secret of the Student's sorrow, and she sat silent in the oak-tree, and thought about the mystery of Love.

Suddenly she spread her brown wings for flight, and soared into the air. She passed through the grove like a shadow, and like it shadow she sailed across the garden.

In the centre of the grass-plot was standing it beautiful rose-tree, and when she saw it she flew over to it, and lit upon a spray.

'Give me a red rose,' she cried, 'and I will sing you my sweetest song.'

But the Tree shook its head.

'My roses are white,' it answered; as white as the foam of the sea, and whiter than the snow upon the mountain. But go to my brother who grows round the old sun-dial, and perhaps he will give you what you want.'

So the Nightingale flew over to the rose-tree that was growing round the old sun-dial.

'Give me a red rose,' she cried, 'and I will sing you my sweetest song.'

But the Tree shook its head.

'My roses are yellow,' it answered; 'as yellow as the hair of the mermaiden who sits upon an amber throne, and yellower than the daffodil that blooms in the meadow before the mower comes with his scythe. But go to my brother who grows beneath the Student's window, and perhaps he will give you what you want.'

So the Nightingale flew over to the rose-tree that was growing beneath the Student's window.

'Give me a red rose,' she cried, 'and I will sing you my sweetest song.'

But the Tree shook its head.

'My roses are red,' it answered; 'as red as the feet of the dove, and redder than the great fans of coral that wave and wave in the ocean-cavern. But the winter has chilled my veins, and the frost has nipped my buds, and the storm has broken my branches, and I shall have no roses at all this year.'

'One red rose is all I want,' cried the Nightingale, 'only one red rose! Is there no way by which I can get it.

'There is a way,' answered the Tree; 'but it is so terrible that I dare not tell it to you.'

'Tell it to me,' said the Nightingale, 'I am not afraid.'

'It you want a red rose,' said the Tree, 'you must build it out of music by moonlight, and stain it with your own heart's-blood. You must sing to me with your breast against a thorn. All night long you must sing to me, and the thorn must pierce your heart, and your life-blood must flow into my veins, and become mine.'

'Death is it great price to pay for a red rose,' cried the Nightingale, 'and Life is very dear to all. It is pleasant to sit in the green wood, and to watch the Sun in his chariot of gold, and the Moon in her chariot of pearl. Sweet is the scent of the hawthorn, and sweet are the bluebells that hide in the valley, and the heather that blows on the hill. Yet Love is better than Life, and what is the heart of it bird compared to the heart of man?'

So she spread her brown wings for flight, and soared into the air. She swept over the garden like it shadow, and like it shadow she sailed through the grove.

The young Student was still lying on the grass, where she had left him, and the tears were not yet dry in his beautiful eyes.

'Be happy,' cried the Nightingale, 'be happy; you shall have your red rose. I will build it out of music by moonlight, and stain it with my own heart's-blood. All that I ask of you in return is that you will be a true lover, for Love is wiser than Philosophy, though he is wise, and mightier than Power, though he is mighty. Flame-coloured are his wings, and coloured like flame is his body. His lips are sweet as honey, and his breath is like frankincense.'

The Student looked up from the grass, and listened, but he could not understand what the Nightingale was saying to him, for he only knew the things that are written down in books.

But the oak-tree understood, and felt sad, for he was very fond of the little Nightingale who had built her nest in his branches.

'Sing me one last song,' he whispered. 'I shall feel lonely when you are gone.'

So the Nightingale sang to the oak-tree, and her voice was like water bubbling from it silver jar.

When she had finished her song, the Student got up and pulled a note-book and a lead-pencil out of his pocket.

'She has form,' he said to himself, as he walked away through the grove—'that cannot be denied to her; but has she got feeling.' I am afraid not. In fact, she is like most artistes; she is all style without any sincerity. She would not sacrifice herself for others. She thinks merely of music, and everybody knows that the arts are selfish. Still, it must be admitted that she has some beautiful notes in her voice. What a pity it is that they do not mean anything, or do any practical good!' And he went into his room, and lay down on his little pallet-bed, and began to think of his love; and, after a time, he fell asleep.

And when the moon shone in the heavens, the Nightingale flew to the rose-tree, and set her breast against the thorn. All night long she sang, with her breast against the thorn, and the cold crystal Moon leaned down and listened. All night long she sang, and the thorn went deeper and deeper into her breast, and her life-blood ebbed away from her.

She sang first of the birth of love in the heart of it boy and a girl. And on the topmost spray of the rose-tree there blossomed it marvellous rose, petal following petal, as song followed song. Pale was it, at first, as the mist that hangs over the river—pale as the feet of the morning, and silver as the wings of the dawn. As the shadow of a rose in a mirror of silver, as the shadow of a rose in it water-pool, so was the rose that blossomed on the topmost spray of the Tree.

But the Tree cried to the Nightingale to press closer against the thorn. 'Press closer, little Nightingale,' cried the Tree, 'or the Day will come before the rose is finished.'

So the Nightingale pressed closer against the thorn, and louder and louder grew her song, for she sang of the birth of passion in the soul of a man and a maid.

And a delicate flush of pink came into the leaves of the rose, like the flush in the face of the bridegroom when he kisses the lips of the bride. But the thorn had not yet reached her heart, so the rose's heart remained white, for only a Nightingale's heart's—blood can crimson the heart of a rose.

And the Tree cried to the Nightingale to press closer against the thorn. 'Press closer, little Nightingale,' cried the Tree, 'or the Day will come before the rose is finished.'

So the Nightingale pressed closer against the thorn, and the thorn touched her heart, and it fierce pang of pain shot through her. Bitter, bitter was the pain, and wilder and wilder grew her song, for she sang of the Love that is perfected by Death, of the Love that dies not in the tomb.

And the marvellous rose became crimson, like the rose of

the eastern sky. Crimson was the girdle of petals, and crimson as a ruby was the heart.

But the Nightingale's voice grew fainter, and her little wings began to beat, and a film came over her eyes. Fainter and fainter grew her song, and she felt something choking her in her throat.

Then she gave one last burst of music. The white Moon heard it, and she forgot the dawn, and lingered on in the sky. The red rose heard it, and it trembled all over with ecstasy, and opened its petals to the cold morning air. Echo bore it to her purple cavern in the hills, and woke the sleeping shepherds from their dreams. It floated through the reeds of the river, and they carried its message to the sea.

'Look, look!' cried the Tree, 'the rose is finished now'; but the Nightingale made no answer, for she was lying dead in the long grass, with the thorn in her heart.

And at noon the Student opened his window and looked out. 'Why, what a wonderful piece of luck!' he cried; 'here is a red rose! I have never seen any rose like it in all my life. It is so beautiful that I am sure it has a long Latin name'; and he leaned down and plucked it.

Then he put on his hat, and ran up to the Professor's house with the rose in his hand.

The daughter of the Professor was sitting in the doorway winding blue silk on a reel, and her little dog was lying at her feet.

'You said that you would dance with me if I brought you a red rose,' cried the Student. 'Here is the reddest rose in all the world. You will wear it tonight next to your heart, and as we dance together it will tell you how I love you.'

But the girl frowned.

'I am afraid it will not go with my dress,' she answered; 'and, besides, the Chamberlain's nephew has sent me some real jewels, and everybody knows that jewels cost far more than flowers.'

'Well, upon my word, you are very ungrateful,' said the Student angrily; and he threw the rose into the street, where it fell into the gutter, and a cart-wheel went over it. 'Ungrateful!' said the girl. 'I tell you what, you are very rude; and, after all, who are you? Only a Student. Why, I don't believe you have even got silver buckles to your shoes as the Chamberlain's nephew has'; and she got up from her chair and went into the house.

'What a silly thing Love is!' said the Student as he walked away. 'It is not half as useful as Logic, for it does not prove anything, and it is always telling one of things that are not going to happen, and making one believe things that are not true. In fact, it is quite unpractical, and, as in this age to be practical is everything, I shall go back to Philosophy and study Metaphysics.'

So he returned to his room and pulled out a great dusty book, and began to read.

MY TREES IN THE HIMALAYAS

Ruskin Bond

Living in a cottage at 7,000 feet in the Garhwal Himalayas, I am fortunate to have a big window that opens out on the forest so that the trees are almost within my reach. If I jumped, I could land quite neatly in the arms of an oak or horse chestnut. I have never made that leap, but the big langurs—silver-gray monkeys with long, swishing tails—often spring from the trees onto my corrugated tin roof, making enough noise to frighten all the birds away.

Standing on its own outside my window is a walnut tree, and truly this is a tree for all seasons. In winter the branches are bare, but beautifully smooth and rounded. In spring each limb produces a bright green spear of new growth, and by midsummer the entire tree is in leaf. Toward the end of the monsoon the walnuts, encased in their green jackets, have reached maturity. When the jackets begin to split, you can see the hard brown shells of the nuts, and inside each shell is the delicious meat itself.

Every year this tree gives me a basket of walnuts. But last year the nuts were disappearing one by one, and I was at a loss as to who had been taking them. Could it have been the milkman's small son? He was an inveterate tree climber, but he was usually to be found on the oak trees, gathering fodder for his herd. He admitted that his cows had enjoyed my dahlias, which they had eaten the previous week, but he stoutly denied having fed them walnuts.

It wasn't the woodpecker either. He was out there every day, knocking furiously against the bark of the tree, trying to pry an insect out of a narrow crack, but he was strictly non-vegetarian. As for the langurs, they ate my geraniums but did not care for the walnuts.

The nuts seemed to disappear early in the morning while I was still in bed, so one day I surprised everyone, including myself by getting up before sunrise. I was just in time to catch the culprit climbing out of the walnut tree. She was an old woman who sometimes came to cut grass on the hillside. Her face was as wrinkled as the walnuts she so fancied, but her arms and legs were very sturdy.

'And how many walnuts did you gather today, Grandmother?' I asked.

'Just two,' she said with a giggle, offering them to me on her open palm. I accepted one, and thus encouraged, she climbed higher into the tree and helped herself to the remaining nuts. It was impossible for me to object. I was taken with admiration for her agility. She must have been twice my age, but I knew I could never get up that tree. To the victor, the spoils!

Unlike the prized walnuts, the horse chestnuts are inedible. Even the rhesus monkeys throw them away in disgust. But the tree itself is a friendly one, especially in summer when it is in full leaf. The lightest breeze makes the leaves break into conversation, and their rustle is a cheerful sound. The spring flowers of the horse chestnut look like candelabra, and when the blossoms fall, they carpet the hillside with their pale pink petals.

It stands erect and dignified and does not bend with the wind. In spring the new leaves, or needles, are a tender green, while during the monsoon the tiny young cones spread like blossoms in the dark green folds of the branches. The deodar enjoys the company of its own kind: where one deodar grows, there will be others. A walk in a deodar forest is awe-inspiring—surrounded on all sides by these great sentinels of the mountains, you feel as though the trees themselves are on the march.

I walk among the trees outside my window often, acknowledging their presence with a touch of my hand against their trunks. The oak has been there the longest, and the wind has bent its upper branches and twisted a few so that it looks shaggy and undistinguished. But it is a good tree for the privacy of birds. Sometimes it seems completely uninhabited until there is a whining sound, as of a helicopter approaching, and a party of long-tailed blue magpies flies across the forest glade.

Most of the pines near my home are on the next hillside. But there is a small Himalayan blue one a little way below the cottage, and sometimes I sit beneath it to listen to the wind playing softly in its branches.

When I open the window at night, there is almost always something to listen to—the mellow whistle of a pygmy owlet, or the sharp cry of a barking deer. Sometimes, if I am lucky, I will see the moon coming up over the next mountain, and two distant deodars in perfect silhouette.

Some night sounds outside my window remain strange and mysterious. Perhaps they are the sounds of the trees themselves, stretching their limbs in the dark, shifting a little, flexing their fingers, whispering to one another. These great trees of the mountains, I feel they know me well, as I watch them and listen to their secrets, happy to rest my head beneath their outstretched arms.

THE GIFT OF THE MAGI

O. Henry

One dollar and eighty-seven cents. That was all. And sixty cents of it was in pennies. Pennies saved one and two at a time by bulldozing the grocer and the vegetable man and the butcher until one's cheek burned with the silent imputation of parsimony that such close dealing implied. Three times Della counted it. One dollar and eighty-seven cents. And the next day would be Christmas.

There was clearly nothing left to do but flop down on the shabby little couch and howl. So Della did it. Which instigates the moral reflection that life is made up of sobs, sniffles and smiles, with sniffles predominating.

While the mistress of the home is gradually subsiding from the first stage to the second, take a look at the home. A furnished flat at $8 per week. It did not exactly beggar description, but it certainly had that word on the look-out for the mendicancy squad.

In the vestibule below was a letter-box into which no letter would go, and an electric button from which no mortal finger could coax a ring. Also appertaining thereunto was a card bearing the name 'Mr James Dillingham Young.'

The 'Dillingham' had been flung to the breeze during a former period of prosperity when its possessor was being paid $30 per week. Now, when the income was shrunk to $20, the letters of 'Dillingham' looked blurred, as though they were thinking seriously of contracting to a modest and unassuming D. But whenever Mr James Dillingham Young came home and reached his flat above he was called 'Jim' and greatly hugged by Mrs James Dillingham Young, already introduced to you as Della. Which is all very good.

Della finished her cry and attended to her cheeks with the powder rag. She stood by the window and looked out dully at a grey cat walking a grey fence in it grey backyard. Tomorrow would be Christmas Day, and she had only $1.87 with which to buy Jim a present. She had been saving every penny she could for months, with this result. Twenty dollars a week doesn't go far. Expenses had been greater than she had calculated. They always are. Only $1.87 to buy a present for Jim. Her Jim. Many a happy hour she had spent planning for something nice for him. Something fine and rare and sterling—something just a little bit near to being worthy of the honour of being owned by Jim.

There was a pier-glass between the windows of the room. Perhaps you have seen a pier-glass in an $8 flat. A very thin and very agile person may, by observing his reflection in a rapid sequence of longitudinal strips, obtain a fairly accurate conception of his looks. Della, being slender, had mastered the art.

Suddenly she whirled from the window and stood before the glass. Her eyes were shining brilliantly, but her face had lost its colour within twenty seconds. Rapidly she pulled down her hair and let it fall to its full length.

Now, there were two possessions of the James Dillingham Youngs in which they both took a mighty pride. One was Jim's gold watch that had been his father's and his grandfather's. The other was Della's hair. Had the Queen of Sheba lived in the flat across the airshaft, Della would have let her hair hang out the window some day to dry just to depreciate Her Majesty's jewels and gifts. Had King Solomon been the janitor, with all his treasures piled up in the basement, Jim would have pulled out his watch every time he passed, just to see him pluck at his beard from envy.

So now Della's beautiful hair fell about her, rippling and shining like a cascade of brown waters. It reached below her knee and made itself almost a garment for her. And then she did it up again nervously and quickly. Once she faltered for a minute and stood still while a tear or two splashed on the worn red carpet.

On went her old brown jacket; on went her old brown hat. With a whirl of skirts and with the brilliant sparkle still in her eyes, she fluttered out of the door and down the stairs to the street.

Where she stopped the sign read: 'Mme. Sofronie. Hair Goods of All Kinds.' One flight up Della ran, and collected herself, panting. Madame, large, too white, chilly, hardly looked the 'sofronie'.

'Will you buy my hair?' asked Della.

'I buy hair,' said Madame. 'Take yer hat off and let's have a sight at the looks of it.'

Down rippled the brown cascade.

'Twenty dollars,' said Madame, lifting the mass with a practised hand.

'Give it to me quick,' said Della.

Oh, and the next two hours tripped by on rosy wings.

Forget the hashed metaphor. She was ransacking the stores for Jim's present.

She found it at last. It surely had been made for Jim and no one else. There was no other like it in any of the stores, and she had turned all of them inside out. It was a platinum fob chain simple and chaste in design, properly proclaiming its value by substance alone and not by meretricious ornamentation—as all good things should do. It was even worthy of the Watch. As soon as she saw it she knew that it must be Jim's. It was like him. Quietness and value—the description applied to both. Twenty-one dollars they took from her for it, and she hurried home with the 87 cents. With that chain on his watch Jim might be properly anxious about the time in any company. Grand as the watch was, he sometimes looked at it on the sly on account of the old leather strap that he used in place of a chain.

When Della reached home her intoxication gave way it little to prudence and reason. She got out her curling irons and lighted the gas and went to work repairing the ravages made by generosity added to love. Which is always a tremendous task, dear friends—a mammoth task.

Within forty minutes her head was covered with tiny, close-lying curls that made her look wonderfully like a truant schoolboy. She looked at her reflection in the mirror long, carefully and critically.

'If Jim doesn't kill me,' she said to herself, 'before he takes it second look at me, he'll say I look like a Coney Island chorus girl. But what could I do—oh! what could I do with it dollar and 87 cents?'

At seven o'clock the coffee was made and the frying-pan was on the back of the stove, hot and ready to cook the chops.

Jim was never late. Della doubled the fob chain in her land

But she hugged them to her bosom, and at length she was able to look up with dim eyes and a smile and say: 'My hair grows so fast, Jim!'

And then Della leaped up like a little singed cat and cried, 'Oh, oh!'

Jim had not yet seen his beautiful present. She held it out to him eagerly upon her open palm. The dull precious metal seemed to flash with a reflection of her bright and ardent spirit.

'Isn't it a dandy, Jim? I hunted all over town to find it. You'll have to look at the time a hundred times a day now. Give me your watch. I want to see how it looks on it.'

Instead of obeying, Jim tumbled down on the couch and put his hands under the back of his head and smiled.

'Dell,' said he, 'let's put our Christmas presents away and keep 'em awhile. They're too nice to use just at present. I sold the watch to get the money to buy your combs. And now suppose you put the chops on.'

The magi, as you know, were wise men—wonderfully wise men—who brought gifts to the Babe in the manger. They invented the art of giving Christmas presents. Being wise, their gifts were no doubt wise ones, possibly bearing the privilege of exchange in case of duplication. And here I have lamely related to you the uneventful chronicle of two foolish children in a flat who most unwisely sacrificed for each other the greatest treasures of their house. But in a last word to the wise of these days, let it be said that of all who give gifts these two were the wisest. Of all who give and receive gifts, such as they are wisest. Everywhere they are wisest. They are the magi.

THE FOLDER

Noel Langley

In the foyer of the Hotel Splendide, the news-stand and the tobacconist are combined in haughty style, sharing a palatial booth of marble and chromium. It is the only commercial note in the foyer; the rest looks like decadent Pompeii at the height of its luxury. The carpets sink submissively beneath your feet like eiderdown; the pillars glisten sleekly; the chairs and sofas look as if only royalty could feel at home in them, and the palms, placed concentrically round the goldfish pool in the centre, lend an air of exotic pomp. Though a ceaseless human stream moves in and out of its august precincts from sunrise to sunrise, the air is always hushed and reverent. The lifts drift effortlessly from the upper floors, open their doors silently, and as silently and unobtrusively glide upwards again, The page-boys never shout; they intone in modulated minor keys. The doors to the street are quilted and soundproof, and you must pass through two sets of them before the world is left behind you, and the Splendide envelops you in its mystic hush.

The Folder

The staff at the Reception Desk resemble and behave li[ke] diplomats. It has been proved psychologically impossible for [a] bad cheque to be passed across their counter. Their restraint a[nd] tone act as a litmus-test upon the acid of a dishonest conscienc[e.] A bogus cheque would shrivel and fall to ashes as it slid acro[ss] the shining counter of the cashier's desk, and invisible, sepulchr[al] bells would toll a requiem for the soul of the imprudent gamble[r] fool enough to have tried it.

It is in the foyer that visitors and friends await audience wit[h] the guests, much as penitents await audience with the Pope[.] The favoured ones are eventually spirited away by a page-boy to be swallowed for ever in the velvet silence of the hotel's inner maw; but the lesser mortals never advance further than the line of demarcation of the palms. They sink uneasily into the chairs and sofas, and put up a pitiful show of being at ease and unabashed by their surroundings; only the more abandoned smoke; and in the days before the war, the rest read periodicals that the hotel supplied in large leather folders with its crest stamped in gold upon the outer flap.

The war having impoverished even the inviolate precincts of the Splendide, the paper shortage having penetrated there as impudently as if the hotel were no better than it should be, many of the folders are now empty vessels, nostalgic reminders of a way of English life that is now rattling in tumbrils to the guillotine.

A Miss Kittering worked in the news-stand, and a Miss Blombell presided over the tobacco. They were on moderately cordial terms, being ladies of refined temperament and sheltered upbringing, but they had their occasional differences. Such matters as the allocation of small change in the cash register, the reading of periodicals by Miss Blombell and the untidying of good-looking and his air was that of respectful equanimity to life in general. His boots were brightly polished, and his hair newly cut and brushed. The brass on him glittered proudly, and only his chainsmoking gave away his inner misgivings.

He had looked wanly though the empty folders in search of something to read, and then sat back and gave himself up to watching the parade of great and near-great that undulated unhurriedly to and from the lifts and the quilted doors.

When he had been there an hour, a family emerged from one of the lifts and coursed majestically towards him. The father and mother were elderly and arrayed in slightly old-fashioned glory, and their daughter, walking a little ahead and looking eagerly about her, was young and pretty and as well-bred as a racehorse. The soldier stood up, and though he kept a pokerface, his adoration flowed through it so palpably that not even a child of five could have been deceived. He and the girl were in love, and were blissfully deluded into thinking they kept it a secret from the world.

The parents were introduced, and the group sat down sedately. Polite conversation came into play, and after a moment or so it was obvious even to Miss Blombell at the far end of the foyer that a steel curtain was lowering itself slowly between the parents and the young man. It could not have been more clear to Miss Blombell that he was being subjected to a grilling examination, and that he was being found not suitable. His shyness took the form of a kind of ingratiating humility; his anxiety to please fell wider and wider of the mark.

The parents could not have been more magnanimous and open-minded. It was clear that their policy was to give him full credit for his assets before they found him wanting in essentials. The girl, watching the effect of his personality on her parents, and theirs on him, for the first time, was obviously giving way to a slow, quiet despair. In the clear light of unsentimental reality, she saw, for the first time, the long complicated vista of incompatibilities that would be their future; the unending readjustments, the two diametric ways of life and thought that would clash and grate and ultimately reach deadlock.

The father took the offensive, and in ponderous and patient idiom slowly asked questions, and added profound comments to the young soldier's answers, nodding sympathetically when some point he had made could not be adequately answered. The idyllic rapture of the young people's love was being scientifically dismantled, hope by hope.

Miss Blombell became so engrossed that she inadvertently sold a casual customer a packet of holy cigarettes from under the counter. At the end of half an hour the issue was no longer a doubtful one. The soldier had been driven from the field, and the parents were hoisting their victorious colours. The girl was pale and quiet; she no longer sought the soldier's glance, thereby to reaffirm his courage for him: she looked down at her gloves, and brushed non-existent creases from her dress, or stared over her father's head at the palms.

Later, Miss Blombell knew, when she was alone, she would cry; because it was all over. The soldier had become stiff and awkward; he faltered now when he answered, and otherwise made no effort to speak; it was obviously taking all his effort to keep his face mask-like. Already sick, numb, despairing ache had routed the joy in his breast.

Miss Blombell felt like a receiving set picking up short-wave emotions; she could almost reduplicate, in her own breast, the feeling of anguish and defeat in the girl. She had a wild, unseemly desire to shout across the foyer, 'Keep your heart up!

Don't let those old fogies get you down!'

The father called a page-boy and ordered drinks—they were to part on civil terms, with all the laws of courtesy and civility respected. The tension relaxed into natural apathy, and the soldier picked up one of the leather folders and opened it idly. He sat for a moment looking at it.

And then, suddenly, his mood began to alter. His body straightened, his head came up. Miss Blombell felt a shiver of excitement run down her spine. The soldier handed the folder silently and casually to the girl, as if it were of no more importance than an ash-tray or a dropped glove; and the girl, taking it with a faintly puzzled air, opened it listlessly. The page-boy left, and the parents returned their attention to the two young people; but it was clear now that a new element had entered into the situation, for suddenly the girl began to talk, slowly at first, but with increasing assurance, and the mother and father changed their positions in their chairs, as if confounded and pained.

Miss Blombell was distracted at this moment by an elderly lady demanding a Havana cigar, and when she was able to catch up with the quartet again, the girl was on the edge of her chair, her head tilted defiantly, and her words came steadily and with authority. The soldier's attitude had changed, too. He leaned forward, and his eyes were fixed on hers with pride and admiration. Occasionally, he darted a glance at her mother and father, but there was nothing down-trodden about him now. It was clear that the parents were struggling to keep their tempers in check to prevent an unseemly exhibition in a public place. The mother had become soothing, and the father's hand waved placatingly, but the tide, having turned, now swept on, and the girl rose suddenly, held out her hand to the soldier, and pulled him towards her. They walked firmly and purposefully through the foyer and out of the quilted doors into the street, and the parents, after an ineffectual flutter, rose and made their way to the lift, talking agitatedly in undertones.

Miss Blombell, elated, removed her spectacles and wiped them. Her heart felt foolishly light and free, as if it were she herself who had flaunted the parents and chosen her own way of life. For a moment she felt ridiculously young. It took a sharp cough from Miss Kittering to bring her back to earth, to attend to a Foreign Office official in need of cigarettes from the secret cache. When her mind had leisure to return to the subject, she began to speculate as to what had been in the folder...

'Miss Kittering,' she said casually, 'did you supply the magazines for the folders on that table over there?'

'Indeed I did not,' Miss Kittering made answer, 'I was unaware of the presence of magazines in the folders.'

'Well, that *is* odd, isn't it?' said Miss Blombell, greatly intrigued, but in no way anxious to share confidences with Miss Kittering. As she spoke, she saw an elderly woman, thumbing aimlessly through the folders, suddenly pause, twitch, and slap the folder shut with a gesture of supercilious irritation.

From then on Miss Blombell never let her eye wander too far from the folders and on the table. The special one lay at the end of the table, and it was easy to keep it under survey. In rough order, it brought reactions of amusement, irritability or bored indifference; but Miss Blombell was convinced that something very odd lay within it.

About half an hour before she went off duty, Colin Mather came in. Even with the shortage of newsprint, Miss Blombell knew all about the Mather divorce, and under her counter she kept twenty cigarettes a day for Mrs Mather, who was living at the Splendide with her two small children. They were a glamorous couple, and in the days before the war the society periodicals ran pictures of them at Ascot, first nights, the Riviera, and sitting on shooting sticks in Scotland. The marriage had gone up in smoke during the war, and they had been separated for nearly a year. They never met except in the company of a lawyer; they were obviously bitter towards each other, and their wounded vanities wrestled for supremacy. Their friends had sided fairly evenly, and clearly neither of them was entirely without blame. Mrs Mather was now receiving attentions from a stately admirer who never proceeded further than the foyer when he called for her or brought her back to the hotel. He was rich and calm and dreary, and Miss Blombell took especial pleasure in pointing to her 'No Cigarettes' sign when he paused at her counter.

Colin Mather, on the other hand, she rather admired. He had been a Commando, and even in civilian clothes cut rather a dash. He had the sort of face that advertise pipe tobacco, and had begun to grey at the temples. Perhaps, he was a little ordinary, too; but not as much so as the new admirer, and Miss Blombell, faithful until then to Mrs Mather's cause, felt her loyalties beginning to shift anchor. A few minutes later Mrs Mather appeared from the lift, followed by her lawyer, and they made their way to where he was standing and exchanged cool, formal greetings. Miss Blombell had observed that Mr Mather had opened and closed the folder casually, just before he saw his wife, and when they sat down he took the chair that the young private had used.

An air of impeccable impartiality hung over them. They were clearly finishing up some trivial agenda to a clause in the divorce suit; they both looked bored and passive, nodding faintly as the lawyer paused for confirmation, and letting their attentions wander with elaborate negligence in any direction save towards each other.

Colin Mather spoke, addressing himself deliberately to the lawyer, and the lawyer hesitated and looked at Mrs Mather for guidance. Mrs Mather replied in quiet and unruffled terms, addressing her husband directly, and wearing the expression of a patient governess. It was apparent that disagreement was now in the air, and though they never betrayed their feelings by expression, or lifted their voices from a casual conversational level, the breach was becoming wider as they spoke; and at last Mrs Mather shrugged resignedly and turned away, and Colin began stubbing out his cigarette as if it had turned on him and bitten his finger. The lawyer's attitude had obviously stiffened, too, and his lips were thin and severe, though he still spoke more in sorrow than in anger.

Colin Mather then began talking in a rapid undertone, clearly pulling at the cupboard door to expose a skeleton or two; and now his wife caught some of his anger and began to reply with equal heat. The lawyer coughed, and they both stopped short, embarrassed. She half rose. The lawyer detained her, and she sat again, unwillingly. The tension refused to abate, however. Her husband, leaning back in exaggerated ease to show himself master of the situation, brushed the folder with his elbow. For a moment his anger grappled with some other emotion. Then he picked up the folder and handed it to her without a word. She took it half-suspiciously, hesitated a moment, and then opened it.

Miss Blombell's view was obscured for a few seconds by a passing group of matrons, and when she could see the trio again, to her amazement Mrs Mather had begun to cry. She pushed the folder back into her husband's hand, and opened her bag in search of a handkerchief. The lawyer looked uncomprehendingly at them both. Colin Mather returned the folder to the table and then slowly and tentatively he held out his hand. Slowly, she put out her own towards him, and for a moment they sat like children, gazing at each other wistfully. Then she rose, still holding his hand, and they walked together towards the lift, leaving the lawyer to his own devices.

Miss Blombell's curiosity was now at fever pitch; she felt she must see what was in the folder before she was another minute older, or scream. But Mrs Platty, who took over when she went off duty, was late, and she was marooned behind her counter.

A cold, thin dowager had paused by the table now, in a fruitless search for a magazine. When she came to the end folder, her brow darkened, and after a moment's private debate she came across the foyer and handed the folder to Miss Kittering.

'You might be interested to know of this vandalism,' she said acidly. 'Someone has been doing some vulgar scrawling in here.'

'I'm afraid I have nothing to do with these folders, madam,' Miss Kittering replied aloofly. 'I suggest that you register your complaint with one of the managers—'

Miss Blombell edged over from her side of the booth and, controlling her eagerness with an effort, held out her hand.

'If you'd care to leave it with me, madam, I'll see that it reaches the manager,' she said politely.

'Some people might think it a matter of small consequence,' said the dowager, handing over the folder, 'but a thing like this can contribute harmfully to disrespect of private property. It's not the sort of thing one expects to find in a hotel of this standard.'

She turned and moved away. Indifferent to Miss Kittering's surprised stare, Miss Blombell opened the folder. It was empty, like the others; but in deeply scored pencil, in large block letters, was written inside its cover, 'I LOVE YOU, LOVE YOU, LOVE YOU SO!'

WHAT HAPPENED TO A FATHER WHO BECAME A SCHOOLBOY

F. Anstey

Perhaps it would be a good thing if some fathers were transformed into boys and went to school again. But perhaps it would not be so good if boys were suddenly changed into heavy-weight seniors. What might happen in both cases was the original idea of an amusing book, Vice Versa: A Lesson to Fathers, by Thomas Anstey Guthrie. The father in Vice Versa, Mr Paul Multitude, was bidding goodbye in a sermonizing way to his son Dick, who was not very keen—at any rate, for the moment—about returning to school. Dick handed his father a curious stone which his Uncle Duke had brought from India, and which had magic powers of fulfilling the first wish expressed by whoever held the stone. Mr Bultitude, as fathers will do, happened to say that he wished he could be like Dick again—and lo! he became a boy. Feeling himself to be in a ridiculous position, he tried to wish himself back to his former self; but the Garuda stone did not work that way. He gave the stone to

Dick, thinking that he might wish things back as they were. But Dick, realising his unique opportunity to escape school, uttered his own wish—and lo! he became Bultitude senior.

'What did you say?' gasped Paul.

'Why, you see,' exclaimed Dick, 'it would never have done for us both to go back; the chaps would have humbugged us so; and as I hate the place, and you seem so fond of being a boy and going back to school and that, I thought perhaps it would be best for you to go and see how you liked it!'

'I never will! I'll not stir from this room! I dare you to try to move me!' cried Paul. And just then there was the sound of wheels outside once more. They stopped before the house, the bell rang sharply—the long-expected cab had come at last.

'You've no time to lose,' said Dick, 'get your coat on.'

Mr Bultitude tried to treat the affair as a joke. He laughed a ghastly little laugh.

'Ha! ha! You've fairly caught your poor old father this time; you've proved him wrong. I admit I said more than I exactly meant. But that's enough. Don't drive a good joke too far; shake hands, and let us see if we can't find a way out of this!'

But Dick only warmed his coat tails at the fire as he said, with a very ungenerous reminiscence of his father's manner: 'You are going back to an excellent establishment, where you will enjoy all the comforts of home—I can particularly recommend the stick jaw; look out for it on Tuesdays and Fridays. You will once more take part in the games and lessons of happy boyhood. (Did you ever play "chevy" before when you were a boy? You'll enjoy "chevy".) And you will find your companions easy enough to get on with, if you don't go giving yourself airs; they won't stand airs. Now goodbye, my boy, and bless you!'

Paul stood staring stupidly at this outrageous assumption; he could scarcely believe even yet that it was meant in cruel earnest. Before he could answer, the door opened and Boaler appeared.

'Had a deal of trouble to find a keb, sir, on a night like this,' he said to the false Dick, 'but the luggage is all on top, and the man says there's plenty of time still.'

'Goodbye then, my boy,' said Dick, with well-assumed tenderness, but a rather dangerous light in his eye. 'Remember, I expect you to work...'

♦

[Mr Paul Bultitude, now transformed into his son, found himself being driven to the station, en route for school. In his unaccustomed surroundings there, he had a bad time—very different from that spent by Dick, according to this letter from Miss Bultitude sent to her supposed brother at the school.]

'My dearest darling Dick, I hope you have not been expecting a letter from me before this, but I had such lots to tell you that I waited till I had time to tell it all at once. For I have such news for you! You can't think how pleased you will be when you hear it. Where shall I begin? I hardly know, for it still seems so funny and strange—almost like a dream—only I hope we shall never wake up.

'I think I must tell you anyhow, just as it comes. Well, ever since you went away (how was it you never came up to say goodbye to us in the drawing-room? We couldn't believe till we heard the door shut that you really had driven away without another word!) Where am I? Oh, ever since you went away, dear

What Happened to a Father Who Became a Schoolboy 33

Papa has been completely changed; you would hardly believe it unless you saw him. He is quite jolly and boyish—only fancy! and we are always telling him he is the biggest baby of us all, but it only makes him laugh. Once, you know, he would have been awfully angry if we had even hinted at it.

'Do you know, I really think that the real reason he was so crabby and sharp with us that last week was because you were going away; for now the wrench of parting is over, he is quite light-hearted again. You know how he always hates showing his feelings.

'He is so altered now, you can't think. He has actually only once been up to the city since you left, and then he came home at four o'clock, and he seems quite like to have us all about him. Generally, he stays at home all the morning and plays at soldiers with baby in the dining room. You would laugh to see him loading the cannons with real powder and shot, and he didn't care a bit when some of it made holes in the sideboard and smashed the looking-glass.

'We had such fun the other afternoon; we played at brigands—Papa and all of us. Papa had the upper conservatory for a robber-cave, and stood there keeping guard with your pop gun; and he wouldn't let the servants go by without a kiss, unless they showed a written pass from us! Miss McFadden called in the middle of it, but she said she wouldn't come in, as Papa seemed to be enjoying himself so. Boaler has given warning, but we can't think why. We have been out nearly every evening—once to Hengler's and once to the Christy Minstrels, and last night to the Pantomime, where papa was so pleased with the clown that he sent round afterwards and asked him to dine here on Sunday, when Sir Benjamin and Lady Bangle and Alderman Fishwick are coming. Won't it be jolly to see a clown so close? Should you think he'd come in his evening dress? Miss Mangnall has been given a month's holiday, because papa didn't like to see us always at lessons. Think of that!

'We are going to have the whole house done up and refurnished at last. Papa chose the furniture for the drawing-room yesterday. It is all in yellow satin, which is rather bright, I think. I haven't seen the carpet yet, but it is to match the furniture; and there is a lovely hearthrug, with a lion-hunt worked on it.

'But that isn't the best of it; we are going to have the big children's party after all! No one but children invited, and everyone to do exactly what they like. I wanted so much to have you home for it, but papa says it would only unsettle you and take you away from your work.

'Had Dulcie forgotten you? I should like to see her so much. Now I really must leave off, as I am going to the Aquarium with papa. Mind you write me as good a letter as this is, if that old Doctor lets you. Minnie and Roly send love and kisses, and papa sends his kind regards, and I am to say he hopes you are settling down steadily to work.'

'With best love, your affectionate sister,'

'Barbara Bultitude.'

◆

[Dulcie, mentioned in the letter, was the headmaster's daughter—between whom and Dick there had been a friendship, which Paul Bultitude of course could not continue. His troubles are complicated by a mischievous girl, who in church passes him a note, believing him to be the Dick of previous terms. The affair is discovered by

the headmaster, who is about to punish the embarrassed
Paul—when Dick, as Bultitude senior, visits the school.]

And still the Doctor lingered. Some kindly suggested that he was 'waxing the cane.' But the more general opinion was that he had been detained by some visitor; for it appeared that (though Paul had not noticed it) several had heard a ring at the bell. The suspense was growing more and more unbearable.

At last the door opened in a slow ominous manner, and the Doctor appeared. There was a visible change in his manner, however. The white heat of his indignation had died out: his expression was grave but distinctly softened—and he had nothing in his hand.

'I want you outside, Bultitude,' he said; and Paul, still uncertain whether, the scene of his disgrace was only about to be shifted, or what else this might mean, followed him into the hall.

'If anything can strike shame and confusion into your soul, Richard,' said the Doctor, when they were outside, 'it will be what I have to tell you now. Your unhappy father is here, in the dining-room.'

Paul staggered. Had Dick, the brazen effrontery, to come here to taunt him in his slavery? What was the meaning of it? What should he say to him? He could not answer the Doctor but by a vacant stare.

'I have not seen him yet,' said the Doctor. 'He has come at a most inopportune moment (here Mr Bultitude could not agree with him). I shall allow you to meet him first, and give you the opportunity of breaking your conduct to him. I know how it will wring his paternal heart,' and the Doctor shook his head sadly, and turned away.

With a curious mixture of shame, anger and impatience, Paul turned the handle of the dining-room door. He was to meet Dick face to face once more. The final duel must be fought out between them here. Who would be the victor?

It was a strange sensation on entering to see the image of what he had so lately been standing by the mantelpiece. It gave a shock to his sense of his own identity. It seemed so impossible that that stout substantial frame could really contain Dick. For an instant he was totally at a loss for words, and stood pale and speechless in the presence of his unprincipled son.

Dick, on his side, seemed at least as much embarrassed. He giggled uneasily, and made a sheepish offer to shake hands, which was indignantly declined.

As Paul looked he saw distinctly that his son's fraudulent imitation of his father's personal appearance had become deteriorated in many respects since that unhappy night when he had last seen it. It was then a copy, faultlessly accurate in every detail. It was now almost a caricature, a libel!

The complexion was nearly sallow, with the exception of the nose, which had rather deepened in colour. The skin was loose and flabby, and the eyes dull and a little bloodshot. But, perhaps, the greatest alteration was in the dress. Dick wore an old light tweed shooting-coat of his, and a pair of loose trousers of blue serge; while, instead of the formally tied black neckcloth his father had worn for a quarter of a century, he had a large scarf round his neck of some crude and gaudy colour; and the conventional chimney-pot hat had been discarded for a shabby old wide-brimmed felt wide-awake.

Altogether, it was by no means the costume which a British merchant, with any self-respect whatever, would select, even for a country visit.

And thus they met, as perhaps never, since this world was first set spinning down the ringing grooves of change, met father and son before!

Paul was the first to break a very awkward silence. 'You young scoundrel!' he said, with suppressed rage. 'What the devil do you mean by laughing like that? It's no laughing matter, let me tell you, sir, for one of us!'

'I can't help laughing,' said Dick, 'you do look so queer!'

'Queer! I may well look queer. I tell you that I have never, never in my whole life, spent such a perfectly infernal week as this last!'

'Ah!' observed Dick, 'I thought you wouldn't find it all jam! And yet you seemed to be enjoying yourself, too,' he said with a grin, 'from that letter you wrote.'

'What made you come here? Couldn't you be content with your miserable victory, without coming down to crow and jeer at me?'

'It is not that,' said Dick. 'I—I thought I should like to see the fellows, and find out how you were getting on, you know.' These, however, were not his only and principal motives. He had come down to get a sight of Dulcie.

'Well, sir,' said Mr Bultitude, with ponderous sarcasm, 'you'll be delighted to hear that I'm getting on uncommonly well—oh, uncommonly! Your high-spirited young friends batter me to sleep with slippers on most nights, and, as a general thing, kick me about during the day like a confounded football! And last night, sir, I was going to be expelled; and this morning I'm forgiven, and sentenced to be soundly flogged before the whole school! It was just about to take place as you came in; and I've every reason to believe it is merely postponed!'

'I say, though,' said Dick, 'you must have been going it

rather, you know. I've never been expelled. Has Chawner been sneaking again? What have you been up to?'

'Nothing I solemnly swear—nothing! They're finding out things you've done, and thrashing me.'

'Well,' said Dick soothingly, 'you'll work them all off during the term, I daresay. There aren't many really bad ones. I suppose he's seen my name cut on his writing table?'

'No, not that I'm aware of,' said Paul.

'Oh, he'd let you hear of it if he had!' said Dick. 'It's good for a whacking, that is. But, after all, what's a whacking? I never cared for a whacking.'

'But I do care, sir. I care very much, and, I tell you, I won't stand it. I can't! Dick,' he said abruptly, as a sudden hope seized him. 'You, you haven't come down here to say you're tired of your folly, have you? Do you want to give it up?'

'Rather not,' said Dick. 'Why should I? No school, no lessons, nothing to do but amuse myself, eat and drink what I like, and lots of money. It's not likely, you know.'

'Have you ever thought that you're bringing yourself within reach of the law, sir?' said Paul, trying to frighten him. 'Perhaps you don't know that there's an offence known as "false personation with intent to defraud," and that it's a felony. That's what you're doing at this moment, sir!'

'Not any more than you are!' retorted Dick. 'I never began it. I had as much right to wish to be you, as you had to wish to be me. You're just what you said you wanted to be, so you can't complain.'

'It's useless to argue with you, I see,' said Paul. 'And you've no feelings. But I'll warn you of one thing. Whether that is my body or not you've fraudulently taken possession of, I don't know; if it is not, it is very like mine, and I tell you this about it. The sort of life you're leading it, sir, will very soon make an end of you, if you don't take care. Do you think that a constitution at my age can stand sweet wines and pastry, and late hours? Why, you'll be laid up with gout in another day or two. Don't tell me, sir. I know you're suffering from indigestion at this very minute. I can see your liver (it may be my liver for anything I know) is out of order. I can see it in your eyes.'

Dick was a little alarmed at this, but he soon said: 'Well, and if I am seedy, I can get Barbara to take the stone and wish me all right again. Can't I? That's easy enough, I suppose?'

'Oh, easy enough!' said Paul, with a suppressed groan. 'But, Dick, you don't go up to Mincing Lane in that suit and that hat? Don't tell me you do that!'

'When I do go up, I wear them,' said Dick composedly. 'Why not? It's a roomy suit, and I hate a great topper on my head; I've had enough of that here on Sundays. But it's slow up at your office. The chaps there aren't half up to any larks. I made a first-rate booby-trap, though, one day for an old yellow buffer who came in to see you. He was in a bait when he found the waste-paper basket on his head!'

'What was his name?' said Paul, with forced calm.

'Something like "Shells". He said he was a very old friend of mine, and I told him he lied.'

'Shellack—my Canton correspondent—a man I was anxious to be of use to when he came over!' moaned Mr Multitude. 'Miserable young cub, you don't know what mischief you've done!'

'Well, it won't matter much to you now,' said Dick; 'you're out of it all.'

'Do you—do you mean to keep me out of it forever then?'

asked Paul.

'As long as I ever can!' returned Dick frankly. 'It will be rather interesting to see what sort of a fellow you'll grow into—if you ever do grow. Perhaps you will always be like that, you know. This magic is a rum thing to meddle with.'

There was a pause, in which the conversation seemed about to flag hopelessly, but at last Dick said, almost as if he felt some compunction for his present unfilial attitude: 'Now, you know, it's much better to take things quietly. It can't be altered now, can it? And it's not such bad fun being a boy after all—for some things. You'll get into it by-and-by, you see if you don't, and be as jolly as a sand-boy. We shall get along all right together, too. I shan't be hard on you. It is not my fault that you happen to be at this particular school—you chose it! And after this term you can go to any other school you like—Eton or Rugby, or anywhere. I don't mind the expense. Or, if you'd rather, you can have a private tutor. And I'll buy you a pony, and you can ride in the Row. You shall have a much better time of it than I ever had, as long as you let me go on my own way.'

But these dazzling bribes had no influence upon Mr Bultitude; nothing short of complete restitution would ever satisfy him, and he was too proud and too angry at his crushing defeat to even pretend to be in the least pacified.

'I don't want your pony,' he said bitterly; 'I might as well have a white elephant, and I don't suppose I should enjoy myself much more at a public school than I do here. Let's have no humbug, sir. You're up and I'm down—there's no more to be said—I shall tell the Doctor nothing, but I warn you, if ever the time comes—'

'Oh, of course,' said Dick, feeling tolerably secure, now he had disposed of the main difficulty. 'If you can turn me out, I suppose you will—that's only fair. I shall take care not to give you the chance. And, oh, I say, do you want any tin? How much have you got left?'

Paul turned away his head, lest Dick should see the sudden exultation he knew it must betray, as he said, with an effort to appear unconcerned, 'I came away with exactly five shillings, and I haven't a penny now!'

'I say,' said Dick, 'you are a fellow; you must have been going it. How did you get rid of it all in a week?'

'It went, as far as I can understand,' said Mr Bultitude, 'in rabbits and mice. Some boys claimed it as money they paid you to get them, I believe.'

'All your own fault,' said Dick, 'you would have them drowned. But you'd better have some tin to get along with. How much do you want? Will half-a-crown do?'

'Half-a-crown is not much, Dick,' said his father, almost humbly.

'It's—ahem—a handsome allowance for a young fellow like you,' said Dick, rather unkindly; 'but I haven't any half-crowns left. I must give you this, I suppose.'

And he held out a sovereign, never dreaming what it signified to Paul, who clutched it with feelings too great for words, though gratitude was not a part of them, for was it not his own money?

'And now look out,' said Dick, 'I hear Grim. Remember what I told you; keep it up.'

Dr Grimstone came in with the air of a man who has a painful duty to perform; he started slightly as his eyes noted the change in his visitor's dress and appearance. 'I hope,' he began gravely, 'that your son has spared me the pain of going into the details of his misbehaviour; I wish I could give you a better report of him.'

Dick was plainly, in spite of his altered circumstances, by no means at ease in the schoolmaster's presence; he stood, shifting from foot to foot on the hearthrug, turning extremely red and obstinately declining to raise his eyes from the ground.

'Oh, ah,' he stammered at last, 'you were just going to whack him, weren't you, when I turned up, sir?'

'I found myself forced,' said the Doctor, slightly shocked at this coarse way of putting things, 'to contemplate administering to him (for his ultimate benefit) a sharp corrective in the presence of his school-fellows. I distress you, I see, but the truth must be told. He has no doubt confessed his fault to you?'

'No,' said Dick, 'he hasn't, though. What's he been up to now?'

'I had hoped he would have been more open, more straightforward, when confronted with the father who has proved himself so often indulgent and anxious for his improvement; it would have been a more favourable symptom, I think. Well, I must tell you myself. I know too well what a shock it will be to your scrupulously sensitive moral code, my dear Mr Bultitude (Dick showed a painful inclination to giggle here); but I have to break to you the melancholy truth that I detected this unhappy boy in the act of conducting a secret and amorous correspondence with a young lady in a sacred edifice!'

Dick whistled sharply: 'Oh, I say!' he cried, 'that's bad' (and he wagged his head reprovingly at his disgusted father, who longed to denounce his hypocrisy, but dared not); 'that's bad...he shouldn't do that sort of thing, you know, should he? At his age too...the young dog!'

'This horror is what I should have expected from you,' said the Doctor (though he was in truth more than scandalized by the composure with which his announcement was received). Such boldness is indeed characteristic of the dog, an animal which, as you are aware, was with the ancients a synonym for shamelessness. No boy, however abandoned, should hear such words of unequivocal condemnation from a father's lips without a pang of shame!'

Paul was only just able to control his rage by a great effort.

'You're right there, sir,' said Dick; 'he ought to be well ragged for it...he'll break my heart, if he goes on like this, the young beggar. But we musn't be too hard on him, eh? After all, it's nature, you know, isn't it?'

'I beg your pardon?' said Dr Grimstone very stiffly.

'I mean,' explained Dick, with a perilous approach to digging the other in the ribs, 'we did much the same sort of thing in our time, eh? I'm sure I did—lots of times!'

'I can't reproach myself on that head, Mr Bultitude; and permit me to say, that such a tone of treating the affair is apt to destroy the effect, the excellent moral effect, of your most impressively conveyed indignation just now. I merely give you a hint, you understand!'

'Oh, ah,' said Dick, feeling that he had made a mistake, 'yes, I didn't mean that. But I say, you haven't given him a—a whopping yet, have you?'

'I had just stepped out to procure a cane for that purpose,' said the Doctor, 'when your name was announced.'

'Well, look here, you won't want to start again when I'm gone, will you?'

'An ancient philosopher, my dear sir, was accustomed to postpone the correction of his slaves until the first glow of his indignation had passed away. He found then that he could—'

'Lay it on with more science,' suggested Dick, while Paul

writhed where he stood. 'Perhaps so, but you might forgive him now, don't you think? He won't do it again. If he goes writing any more love-letters, tell me, and I'll come and talk to him; but he's had a lesson, you know. Let him off this time.'

'I have no right to resist such an entreaty,' said the Doctor, 'though I may be inclined myself to think that a few strokes would render the lesson more permanent. I must ask you to reconsider your plea for his pardon.'

Paul heard this with indescribable anxiety; he had begun to feel tolerably sure that his evil hour was postponed *sine die*, but might not Dick be cruel and selfish enough to remain neutral, or even side with the enemy, in support of his assumed character?

Luckily he was not. 'I'd rather let him off,' he said awkwardly; 'I don't approve of caning fellows myself. It never did me any good, I know, and I got enough of it to tell.'

'Well, well, I yield. Richard, your father has interceded for you; and I cannot disregard his wishes, though I have my own view in the matter. You will hear no more of this disgraceful conduct, sir, unless you do something to recall it to my memory. Thank your father for his kindness, which you so little deserved, and take your leave of him.'

'Oh, there, it's all right!' said Dick; 'he'll behave himself after this, I know. And oh! I say, sir,' he added hastily, 'is—is Dulcie anywhere about?'

'My daughter?' asked the Doctor. 'Would you like to see her?'

'I shouldn't mind,' said Dick, blushing furiously.

'I'm sorry to say she has gone out for a walk with her mother,' said the Doctor. 'I'm afraid she cannot be back for some time. It's unfortunate.'

Dick's face fell. 'It doesn't matter,' he muttered awkwardly.

'She's all right, I hope?'

'She is very seldom ailing, I'm happy to say; just now she is particularly well, thank you.'

'Oh, is she?' said Dick gloomily, probably disappointed to find that he was so little missed, and not suspecting that his father had been accepted as a substitute.

'Well, do you mind—could I see the fellows again for a minute or two. I mean I should rather like to inspect the school, you know.'

'See my boys? Certainly, my dear sir, by all means; this way,' and he took Dick out to the schoolroom—Paul following out of curiosity. 'You'll find us at our studies, you see,' said the Doctor, as he opened the first baize door. There was a suspicious hubbub and hum of voices from within; but as they entered every boy was bent over his books with the rapt absorption of the devoted student—an absorption that was the direct effect of the sound the door-handle made in turning.

'Our workshop,' said the Doctor airily, looking around. 'My first form, Mr Bultitude. Some good workers here, and some idle ones.'

Dick stood in the doorway, looking (if the truth must be told) uncommonly foolish. He had wanted, in coming there, to enjoy the contrast between the past and present—which accounts for a good many visits of 'old boys' to the scene of their education. But, confronted with his former schoolfellows, he was seized at first with an utterly unreasonable fear of detection.

The class behaved as classes usually do on such occasions. The good boys smirked and the bad ones stared—the general expression being one of uneasy curiosity. Dick never said a word, feeling strangely bashful and nervous.

'This is Tipping, my Head Boy,' touching that young

gentleman on the shoulder, and making him several degrees more uncomfortable. 'I expect solid results from Tipping some day.'

'He looks as if his head was pretty solid,' said Dick, who had once cut his knuckles against it.

'My second boy, Biddlecomb. If he applies himself, he too will do me credit in the world.'

'How do you do, Biddlecomb?' said Dick. 'I owe you nine-pence—I mean—oh, hang it, here's a shilling for you! Hallo, Chawner!' he went on, gradually overcoming his first nervousness, 'how are you getting on, eh? Doing much in the sneaking way, lately?'

'You know him!' exclaimed the Doctor with naive surprise.

'No, no; I don't know him. I've heard of him, you know—heard of him!' Chawner looked down his nose with a feeble attempt at a gratified simper, while his neighbours giggled with furtive relish.

'Well,' said Dick at last, after a long look at all the old familiar objects, 'I must be off, you know. Got some important business at home this evening to look after. The fellows look very jolly and content, and all that sort of thing. Enough to make one want to be a boy again almost, eh? Goodbye, you chaps—ahem, young gentlemen, I wish you good morning!'

And he went out, leaving behind him the impression that 'young Bultitude's governor wasn't such a bad old buffer.'

He paused at the open front door, to which Paul and the Doctor had accompanied him. 'Goodbye,' he said;

'I wish I'd seen Dulcie. I should like to see your daughter, sir; but it can't be helped. Goodbye; and you—,' he added in a lower tone to his father, who was standing by, inexpressibly pained and disgusted by his utter want of dignity, 'you mind what I told you. Don't try any games with me!'

And, as he skipped jauntily down the steps to the gateway, the Doctor followed his unwieldy, oddly-dressed form with his eyes, inclining his head gravely to Dick's sweeping wave of the hand, asked with a compassionate tone in his voice, 'You don't happen to know, Richard, my boy, if your father has had any business troubles lately—anything to disturb him?'

And Mr Bultitude's feelings prevented him from making any intelligible reply.

[After more troubles at school, Paul Bultitude runs away, and arrives at his home—to find Dick not too happy in the freedom of his strange seniority and about to make an awful mess of things as the paternal man of business. By a strange turn, the Garuda stone is made to perform its magic again; and Paul and Dick become their former selves, father and son—to their mutual satisfaction.]

–F. Anstey (Guthrie): *Vice Versa* (1882).

THE BEGGAR

Anton Chekhov

'Kind sir, have pity; turn your attention to a poor, hungry man! For three days I have had nothing to eat; I haven't five copecks for a lodging, I swear it before God. For eight years I was a village schoolteacher and then I lost my place through intrigues. I fell a victim to calumny. It is a year now since I have had anything to do—'

The advocate Skvortsoff looked at the ragged, fawn-coloured overcoat of the suppliant, at his dull, drunken eyes, at the red spot on either cheek, and it seemed to him as if he had seen this man somewhere before.

'I have now had an offer of a position in the province of Kaluga,' the mendicant went on, 'but I haven't the money to get there. Help me kindly; I am ashamed to ask, but—I am obliged to by circumstances.'

Skvortsoff's eyes fell on the man's overshoes, one of which was high and the other low, and he suddenly remembered something.

'Look here, it seems to me I met you the day before yesterday in Sadovaya Street,' he said; 'but you told me then that you were a student who had been expelled, and not a village schoolteacher. Do you remember?'

'N-no, that can't be so,' mumbled the beggar, taken aback. 'I am a village schoolteacher, and if you like I can show you my papers.'

'Have done with lying! You called yourself a student and even told me what you had been expelled for. Don't you remember?' Skvortsoff flushed and turned from the ragged creature with an expression of disgust.

'This is dishonesty, my dear sir!' he cried angrily. 'This is swindling! I shall send the police for you, damn you! Even if you are poor and hungry, that does not give you any right to lie brazenly and shamelessly!'

The waif caught hold of the door-handle and looked furtively round the antechamber, like a detected thief.

'I—I'm not lying—' he muttered. 'I can show you my papers.' 'Who would believe you?' Skvortsoff continued indignantly. 'Don't you know that it's a low, dirty trick to exploit the sympathy which society feels for village schoolteachers and students? It's rivolting!'

Skvortsoff lost his temper and began to berate the mendicant unmercifully. The impudent lying of the ragamuffin offended what he, Skvortsoff, most prized in himself: his kindness, his tender heart, his compassion for all unhappy beings. That lie, an attempt to take advantage of the pity of its 'subject' seemed to him to profane the charity which he liked to extend to the poor out of the purity of his heart. At first the waif continued to protest innocence, but soon lie grew silent and hung his head in confusion.

'Sir!' he said, laying his hand on his heart, 'the fact is I—was lying! I am neither a student nor a schoolteacher. All that was a fiction. Formerly, I sang in a Russian choir and was sent away for drunkenness. But what else can I do? I can't get along without lying. No one will give me anything when I tell the truth. With truth a man would starve to death or die of cold for lack of a lodging. You reason justly, I understand you, but—what can I do?'

'What can you do? You ask what you can do?' cried Skvortsoff, coming close to him. 'Work! That's what you can do! You must work!'

'Work—yes. I know that myself: but where can I find work?'

'By God, you judge harshly!' cried the beggar with a bitter laugh. 'Where can I find manual labour? It's too late for me to be a clerk because in trade one has to begin as a boy; no one would ever take me for a porter because they couldn't order me about; no factory would have me because for that one has to know a trade, and I know none.'

'Nonsense! You always find some excuse! How would you like to chop wood for me?'

'I wouldn't refuse to do that, but in these days even skilled woodcutters find themselves sitting without bread.'

'Huh! You loafers all talk that way. As soon as an offer is made to you, you refuse it. Will you come and chop wood for me?'

'Yes, sir; I will.'

'Very well; we'll soon find out. Splendid—we'll see—'

Skvortsoff hastened along, rubbing his hands, not without a feeling of malice, and called his cook out of the kitchen.

'Here, Olga,' he said, 'take this gentleman into the woodshed and let him chop wood.'

The tatterdemalion scarecrow shrugged his shoulders, as if in perplexity, and went irresolutely after the cook. It was obvious from his gait that he had not consented to go and chop wood because he was hungry and wanted work, but simply from pride and shame, because he had been trapped by his own words. It was obvious, too, that his strength had been undermined by vodka and that he was unhealthy and did not feel the slightest inclination for toil.

Skvortsoff hurried into the dining-room. From its windows one could see the wood-shed and everything that went on in the yard. Standing at the window, Skvortsoff saw the cook and the beggar come out into the yard by the back door and make their way across the dirty snow to the shed. Olga glared wrathfully at her companion, shoved him aside with her elbow, unlocked the shed, and angrily banged the door.

'We probably interrupted the woman over her coffee,' thought Skvortsoff. 'What an ill-tempered creature!'

Next he saw the pseudo-student seat himself on a log and become lost in thought with his red cheeks resting on his fists. The woman flung down an axe at his feet, spat angrily, and, judging from the expression of her lips, began to scold him. The beggar irresolutely pulled a billet of wood toward him, set it up between his feet, and tapped it feebly with the axe. The billet wavered and fell down. The beggar again pulled it to him, blew on his freezing hands, and tapped it with his axe cautiously, as if afraid of hitting his overshoe or of cutting off his finger. The stick of wood again fell to the ground.

Skvortsoff's anger had vanished and he now began to feel a little sorry and ashamed of himself for having set a spoiled, drunken, perchance sick man to work at menial labour in the cold.

'Well, never mind,' he thought, going into his study from the dining-room. 'I did it for his own good.'

An hour later Olga came in and announced that the wood had all been chopped.

'Good! Give him half a rouble,' said Skvortsoff. 'If he wants to he can come back and cut wood on the first day of each month. We can always find work for him.'

On the first of the month the waif made his appearance and again earned half a rouble, although he could barely stand on his legs. From that day on he often appeared in the yard and every time work was found for him. Now he would shovel snow, now put the wood-shed in order, now beat the dust out of rugs and mattresses. Every time he received from twenty to forty copecks, and once, even a pair of old trousers were sent out to him.

When Skvortsoff moved into another house he hired him to help in the packing and hauling of the furniture. This time the waif was sober, gloomy and silent. He hardly touched the furniture, and walked behind the wagons hanging his head, not even making a pretence of appearing busy. He only shivered in the cold and became embarrassed when the carters jeered at him for his idleness, his feebleness, and his tattered, fancy overcoat. After the moving was over Skvortsoff sent for him.

'Well, I see that my words have taken effect,' he said, handing him a rouble. 'Here's for your pains. I see you are sober and have no objection to work. What is your name?'

'Lushkoff.'

'Well, Lushkoff, I can now offer you some other, cleaner employment. Can you write?'

'I can.'

'Then take this letter to a friend of mine tomorrow and

you will be given some copying to do. Work hard, don't drink, and remember what I have said to you. Goodbye!'

Pleased at having put a man on the right path, Skvortsoff tapped Lushkoff kindly on the shoulder and even gave him his hand at parting. Lushkoff took the letter, and from that day forth came no more to the yard for work.

Two years went by. Then one evening, as Skvortsoff was standing at the ticket window of a theatre paying for his seat, he noticed a little man beside him with a coat collar of curly fur and a worn sealskin cap. This little individual timidly asked the ticket seller for a seat in the gallery and paid for it in copper coins.

'Lushkoff, is that you?' cried Skvortsoff, recognizing in the little man his former wood-chopper. 'How are you? What are you doing? How is everything with you?'

'All right. I am a notary now and get thirty-five roubles a month.'

'Thank heaven! That's fine! I am delighted for your sake. I am very, very glad, Lushkoff. You see, you are my godson, in a sense. I gave you a push along the right path, you know. Do you remember what a roasting I gave you, eh? I nearly had you sinking into the ground at my feet that day. Thank you, old man, for not forgetting my words.'

'Thank you, too,' said Lushkoff. 'If I hadn't come to you then I might still be calling myself a teacher or a student to this day. Yes, by flying to your protection I dragged myself out of a pit.'

'I am very glad indeed.'

'Thank you for your kind words and deeds. You talked splendidly to me then. I am very grateful to you and to your cook. God bless that good and noble woman! You spoke finely then. And I shall be indebted to you to my dying day; but, strictly speaking, it was your cook, Olga, who saved me.'

'How is that?'

'Like this. When I used to come to your house to chop wood she used to begin: "Oh, you sot, you! Oh, you miserable creature! There's nothing for you but ruin." And then she would sit down opposite me and grow sad, look into my face and weep. "Oh, you unlucky man! There is no pleasure for you in this world and there will be none in the world to come. You drunkard! You will burn in hell. Oh, you unhappy one!" And so she would carry on, you know, in that strain. I can't tell you how much misery she suffered, how many tears she shed for my sake. But the chief thing was—she used to chop the wood for me. Do you know, sir, that I did not chop one single stick of wood for you? She did it all. Why this saved me, why I changed, why I stopped drinking at the sight of her I can not explain. I only know that, owing to her words and noble deeds a change took place in my heart; she set me right and I shall never forget it. However, it is time to go now; there goes the bell.'

Lushkoff bowed and departed to the gallery.

READING AND BOOKS IN THE VALLEY

Upendra Arora

It's in the air. There is something almost magical about this valley of ours, green and serene, with a delicate web of little rivulets and dry riverbeds strewn like necklaces across its terrain. Tucked in warmly between the great mountain ranges on one side and India's sacred river on the other, Dehra Dun, or the Doon Valley, has always been a source of enchantment for the traveller, many of whom succumbed to the charm and made the valley their home. The Doon Valley was written about centuries ago, when it was a thick orchard of litchi and mango trees, that was traversed by people going further up to the mountains, later when wars were fought, and then, when Guru Ram Rai first set foot here. The history, sociology, geography and anthropology of the valley was extensively documented in books in the nineteenth century by acclaimed British authors because by then, the British had made it their summer home on the way to a cooler Mussoorie. These hooks written by

Williams and Walton are considered as classics today, as they remain comprehensive and authentic texts of reference.

G.R.C. Williams was the first Superintendent of Dehra Dun. His immensely readable account of his times, *Memoir of Dehra Doon* (1872) was perhaps, written when the fountain pen had not come into existence! H.G. Walton recorded his innings in the valley in his hook, *Gazetteer of Dehra Dun* (1911). Mussoorie and Dehra Dun have always shared a cosy co-habitation. Books about the Doon Valley carry exhaustive information about the 'Queen of the Hills', and likewise, hooks about Mussoorie tell about the Doon that was. *The Story of Mussoorie* (1910) by E. Bodycott offers an interesting account of the valley as the British perceived it—they would reach the valley by road and train and then get porters to take them and their belongings on foot up the hills to Mussoorie.

Picturesque landscapes naturally lend themselves to intellectual creativity. The Doon Valley has been a place of retreat for writers, who like to surround themselves within the echoes of their literary imagination. Among contemporary authors who have made an indelible mark on the literary map of writing in the English language in India and those from Dehra Dun, there is a proud list we can boast of, and rightfully so. Pandit Nehru's niece, Nayantara Sahgal is an old resident of Dehra Dun. Her books, *Plans for Departure* and *Rich Like Us* among others, received critical acclaim internationally when they were published and still enjoy a large readership. Students of literature at university level in Uttarakhand and elsewhere are encouraged to study her body of work. In fact, Pandit Nehru wrote a great deal while he was in jail here in Dehra Dun during the freedom struggle. Now, internationally known for his books, I. Allan Sealy also calls the valley his home. He began writing on travel, and his latest novel *Red* has been published internationally. Leading contemporary poet, Arvind Krishna Mehrotra also shares a close association with Dehra Dun and spends time here at his mother's home. Another writer who became well-known for her writings and whose books have recently been reprinted is Nergis Dalal.

Not just Indians, the valley has stolen the hearts of people from across the seas as well, who chose to make the valley their home and went on to pen their experiences. Two authors who come to mind instantly are Lewis King and David Keeling. Lewis led a most incredible life, having travelled the world the crazy way—and having done that, he still chose the valley to build his home and knit a family of the friends he made. His controversial book, *The Twentieth Century Heretic* questions a range of existing notions of time, space and existence. David Keeling, a former member of the British Foreign Service, retired to build an English style cottage in Dehra Dun. The *Asian Age*, carried a weekly column by him where he wrote joyously amusing anecdotes about the valley and its residents, with a typical whiff of witty British humour. His writings have been published as a collection titled *Doon on a Sunday*.

The valley has always been a seat of learning, as it is home to the finest educational institutions in the country. The Indian Military Academy trains young cadets, the Forest Research Institute is at the helm of research in ecological issues in India, the Wildlife Institute of India is internationally acclaimed for its efforts in protecting the flora and fauna of the subcontinent. One of the oldest institutions in the country, the Trignometrical Survey of India (TSI) has its headquarters here. Well-known and highly respected travel writer, Peter Hopkirk, came looking for information at TSI when he was working on his book, *Quest for Kim*. With a little help from this writer, he was able to go around the museum to pay his tributes to the great Indian cartographers and surveyors. His hook praises his visit to the valley. He writes of his memorable experience at TSI and the help he received in making this possible. Henrich Harrer too, in his book, *Seven Years in Tibet* tells of his understanding of life in the valley where he interned during the Second World War.

Apart from the intensely special symbiotic and symbolic relationship the valley has shared with local, national and international authors, there is also a complimentary culture of reading. Our family-run bookstore in Dehra Dun has grown, matured and developed, just like the readers of our town and the town itself. Thirty-five years ago, ours was a little bookstore on the first floor of the two-floor building we are in today. Gradually, we began recording more orders, needed more space, so we moved downstairs, to a room quarter the size of the current bookstore. A few years down, we had an increasing clientele, more books being published, more books being read, more books being ordered. We needed more shelf space, so we bought the shop next to ours, which belonged to a photographer who ran his studio from there. So many hooks after and to this day, we still need more shelf space, for the wide array of subjects we are required to stock, for the various readers who visit our store. While many like the standard page-turners in the bestsellers lists each month, we have an equal number of readers, asking for travel and religion, self-help and muscle building, patriarchy and anarchy. It's all a good sign. As long as people like to read, my grandfather often said to us, there is hope for a better tomorrow.

Our bookstore is a small seed my grandfather planted in Dehra Dun, which my father and his brothers began to run in the years shortly after Independence. The family tree of the bookstore traces back to Ferozpur Cantt in Punjab, where my grandfather ran a very large bookstore and trained us all. Today, my grandfather, Lala Narain Das is considered the founder of the book trade in India. Once he was confident of the training imparted, he sent each boy of the family out to a town in the country, to sow the seed of learning, to nurture it with the values he engrained, and to give back to the society around him.

For my father, just like it was for his father, a book is always like a friend. And, book-lovers thus are all friends. Our bookstore has always been a meeting place for thinking minds, a watering hole for the intellectually thirsty. Over the years, sitting behind the counter at the bookstore, I have had the privilege of meeting most of Dehra Dun's reading (and hence, thinking) public, its new and growing population, its ambitious adolescents and its nostalgic elders. Through these daily interactions, I have felt the pulse of a valley slowly spread its wings and grow into a town, a town that has learnt to adjust to the needs of its citizens and found itself on the national map as a city that has groomed itself, to become the capital of the hill state of Uttarakhand.

The days that I was at college, helping my father run the store after my lectures, there was a film theatre adjacent to our bookstore. It was called the Odeon Cinema and in those days, it ran English films. That was something the residents looked forward to, and before the show, the regulars would drop in at the bookstore to chat, browse and buy their books. We would get the odd phone call from a customer, requesting us to buy tickets for him for the next show because he was running late, or sometimes much before time for the matinee because he didn't want to miss a chance to watch the screening. For a particular customer, we had standing orders to buy two tickets for the first day first show, irrespective of the screening! There were an equal number of people, who initially did not necessary enjoy reading, but because there was time before the film, they would have no option but to wander in and browse and who over time, began visiting the bookstore as a matter of routine, long after the Cinema was broken down and made into the hotel that it is today.

We still have people dropping in, every other day, asking what happened to the Cinema or reminiscing of those simple and enjoyable evenings. These are either people who moved out then to find greener pastures and returned in remembrance of things past or those that have now retired and settled around the valley and visit the bookstore to refresh the memories of their youth spent here. Books about the area that tell the tales of the times that were are very popular. India's well-known author and someone the writer and our bookstore are fortunate to have as a friend, and a well-wisher, Ruskin Bond, first lived in Dehra Dun. His books talk of the verdant valley and of Mussoorie as it once used to be. He has the rare gift of being able to weave stories that appeal to all ages—young children, teenagers, and adults—and thus, his writing has immortalized the valley and the hill station of Mussoorie in the imagination of readers, forever. He is a master storyteller and commands a readership from ages seven to seventy, which is quite rare for contemporary writing in the world today. The valley now shares a very deep association with him, and his hooks not only have a huge readership in Dehra Dun and among visitors to the valley, but also across the country and other parts of the world.

Khushwant Singh, in his famous column, once wrote most judiciously, that the bookshops of a town are the barometer with which we can justly measure the intellectual strength of a city. And, after a book signing function at our bookstore, he carried a mention about it in the preceding week praising our collection of books. He thought, we were better stocked than most other cities he had been to. What better reflection of the valley's citizens than that!

The valley is famous for its educational institutions for the young—public schools like The Doon School and Welhams rank amongst the best and are deeply steeped in history. Their students have gone on to make a name for themselves in various spheres of life. Indira Gandhi used to visit Dehra Dun with her father. Her love for books brought her to our bookstore regularly. Later, she enrolled her sons at The Doon School and would visit our bookstore when she came down to see them. Even when she became Prime Minister and much after that, she chose to order her books from our bookstore. One of the main attributes of our old and cherished relationship with Indira Gandhi was her love for the environment. Since we publish and stock books on ecological issues, she was always keen to encourage and support us to help the larger cause of conservation. She passed her enthusiasm for reading and protection of the environment down to her son Rajiv, who carried on the legacy. He continued to patronize the bookstore much after.

Since teaching and education carry a great emphasis, the valley has always enjoyed an intellectual air. Schools use written literature as a source of study; children are encouraged to learn more through hooks. They are taught to develop the reading habit to widen their knowledge of the world. Since we have educational institutions, we naturally have educationists, and they too, are driven by a quest for learning. Literature, politics, art, defence and military affairs, ecology and environment, anthropology and history are all subjects that have readers.

Dehra Dun has always been home to citizens who perceive the world through the pages of the books they read. It is a place where most people dream of spending their old age, by a cosy fire in winter, huddled on a rocking chair, curled around a book. This is one reason the city has blossomed—retired educationists, environmentalists, government employees and army officials choose Dehra Dun over other cities to settle down in their old age. They bring with them the knowledge and wisdom that experience unfolds-making the city a 'thinking' one, one that is conscientious and mindful. They are aware of its rich natural, architectural and intellectual heritage and work towards preserving it.

Such social activism is not possible without a constant sense of awareness and understanding of the changing times. This is what books and literature provide—and we can proudly boast that in this supersonic age of cyber-rule, our quaint valley of grey hair and green hedges, has three general bookstores and several others that stock other specialized subjects. Most evenings, these bookstores are buzzing with browsers, steaming with debate and discussion.

'That is one of the myriad reasons for the increasing number of tourists to the valley. Since our bookstore is listed in the *Lonely Planet Guide* for India, we often find ourselves providing necessary tourist information about transport, accommodation and food to customers, and quite happily so! The nature of a good bookstore reflects the internal countenance of a city—just like Cambridge and Oxford are both centres of learning that can boast of their bookstores—Cambridge for Heffers' and Oxford for its Blackwells, we find solace in the pride our citizens display in our bookstore.

Dehra Dun has always been a sophisticated town of

thinkers and thinking. It continues to he a town that cherishes a reputation, for its emphasis on education and learning. It is a shiningly optimistic sign for future generations, on this otherwise rather bumpy road of the not-so-distant future of altering forms of information.

THE LITTLE GHOST

Hugh Walpole

I

Ghosts? I looked across the table at Truscott and had a sudden desire to impress him. Truscott has, before now, invited confidences in just that same way, with his flat impassivity, his air of not caring whether you say anything to him or no, his determined indifference to your drama and your pathos. On this particular evening he had been less impassive. He had himself turned the conversation towards spiritualism, seances, and all that world of humbug, as he believed it to be, and suddenly I saw, or fancied that I saw, an real invitation in his eyes, something that made me say to myself: 'Well, hang it all, I've known Truscott for nearly twenty years; I've never shown him the least little bit of my real self; he thinks me a writing money-machine, with no thought in the world besides my brazen serial stories and the yacht that I purchased out of them.'

So I told him this story, and I will do him the justice to say that he listened to every word of it most attentively, although it was far into the evening before I had finished. He didn't seem impatient with all the little details that I gave. Of course, in a ghost story, details are more important than anything else. But was it a ghost story? Was it a story at all? Was it true even in its material background? Now, as I try to tell it again, I can't be sure. Truscott is the only other person who has ever heard it, and at the end of it he made no comment whatever.

It happened long ago, long before the war, when I had been married for about five years, and was an exceedingly prosperous journalist, with a nice little house and two children, in Wimbledon.

I lost suddenly my greatest friend. That may mean little or much as friendship is commonly held, but I believe that most Britishers, most Americans, most Scandinavians, know before they die one friendship at least that changes their whole life experience by its depth and colour. Very few Frenchmen, Italians or Spaniards, very few Southern people at all, understand these things.

The curious part of it in my particular case was that I had known this friend only four or five years before his death, that I had made many friendships both before and since that have endure over much longer periods, and yet this particular friendship had a quality of intensity and happiness that I have never found elsewhere.

Another curious thing was that I met Bond only a few months before my marriage, when I was deeply in love with my wife, and so intensely preoccupied with my engagement that I could think of nothing else. I met Bond quite casually at someone's house. He was a large-boned, broad-shouldered, slow-smiling man with close-cropped hair turning slightly grey, and our meeting was casual; the ripening of our friendship was casual; indeed, the whole affair may be said to have been casual to the very last. It was, in fact, my wife who said to me one day, when we had been married about a year or so; 'Why, I believe you care more for Charlie Bond than for anyone else in the world.' She said it in that sudden, disconcerting, perceptive way that some women have. I was entirely astonished. Of course I laughed at the idea. I saw Bond frequently. He came often to the house. My wife, wiser than many wives, encouraged all my friendships, and she herself liked Charlie immensely. I don't suppose that anyone disliked him. Some men were jealous of him; some men, the merest acquaintances, called him conceited; women were sometimes irritated by him because so clearly he could get on very easily without them; but he had, I think, no real enemy.

How could he have had? His good-nature, his freedom from all jealousy, his naturalness, his sense of fun, the absence of all pettiness, his common sense, his manliness, and at the same time his broad-minded intelligence, all these things made him a most charming personality. I don't know that he shone very much in ordinary society. He was very quiet and his wit and humour came out best with his intimates.

I was the showy one, and he always played up to me, and I think I patronized him a little and thought deep down in my subconscious self that it was lucky for him to have such a brilliant friend, but he never gave a sign of resentment. I believe now that he knew me, with all my faults and vanities and absurdities, far better than anyone else, even my wife, did, and that is one of the reasons, to the day of my death, why I shall always miss him so desperately.

However, it was not until his death that I realized how

close we had been. One November day he came back to his flat, wet and chilled, didn't change his clothes, caught a cold, which developed into pneumonia, and after three days was dead. It happened that week I was in Paris, and I returned to be told on my doorstep by my wife of what had occurred. At first I refused to believe it. When I had seen him a week before he had been in splendid health; with his tanned, rather rough and clumsy face, his clear eyes, no fat about him anywhere, he had looked as though he would live to a thousand, and then when I realized that it was indeed true I did not during the first week or two grasp my loss.

I missed him, of course; was vaguely unhappy and discontented; railed against life, wondering why it was always the best people who were taken and the others left; but I was not actually aware that for the rest of my days things would be different, and that that day of my return from Paris was a crisis in my human experience. Suddenly one morning, walking down Fleet Street, I had a flashing, almost blinding, need of Bond that was like a revelation. From that moment I knew no peace. Everyone seemed to me dull, profitless and empty. Even my wife was a long way away from me, and my children, whom I dearly loved, counted nothing to me at all. I didn't, after that, know what was the matter with me. I lost my appetite, I couldn't sleep, I was grumpy and nervous. I didn't myself connect it with Bond at all. I thought that I was overworked, and when my wife suggested a holiday, I agreed, got a fortnight's leave from my newspaper, and went down to Glebeshire.

Early December is not a bad time for Glebeshire. It is just then the best spot in the British Isles. I knew a little village beyond St Mary's Moor, that I had not seen for ten years, but always remembered with romantic gratitude, and I felt that that was the place for me now.

I changed trains at Polchester and found myself at last in a little jingle driving out to the sea. The air, the wide open moor, the smell of the sea delighted me, and when I reached my village, with its sandy cover and the boats drawn up in two rows in front of a high rocky cave, and when I ate my eggs and bacon in the parlour of the inn overlooking the sea, I felt happier than I had done for weeks past; but my happiness did not last long. Night after night I could not sleep. I began to feel acute loneliness and knew at last in full truth that it was my friend who I was missing, and that it was not solitude I needed, but his company. Easy enough to talk about having his company, but I only truly knew, down here in this little village, sitting on the edge of the green cliff, looking over into limitless sea, that I was indeed never to have his company again. There followed after that a wild, impatient regret that I had not made more of my time with him. I saw myself, in a sudden vision, as I had really been with him, patronizing, indulgent, a little contemptuous of his good-natured ideas. Had I only a week with him now, how eagerly I would show him that I was the fool and not he, that I was the lucky one every time!

One connects with one's own grief the place where one feels it, and before many days had passed I had grown to loathe the little village, to dread, beyond words, the long, soughing groan of the sea as it drew back down the slanting beach, the melancholy wail of the seagulls, the chattering women under my little window. I couldn't stand it. I ought to go back to London, and yet from that, too, I shrank. Memories of Bond lingered there as they did in no other place, and it was hardly fair to my wife and family to give them the company of the dreary, discontented man that I just then was.

And then, just in the way that such things always happen, I found on my breakfast-table one fine morning a forwarded letter. It was from a certain Mrs Baldwin, and, to my surprise, I saw that it came from Glebeshire, but from the top of the county and not its southern end.

John Baldwin was a Stock Exchange friend of my brother's, a rough diamond, but kindly and generous, and not, I believed, very well off. Mrs Baldwin I had always liked, and I think she always like me. We had not met for some little time and I had no idea what had happened to them. Now in her letter she told me that they had taken an old eighteenth-century house on the north coast of Glebeshire, not very far from Drymouth, that they were enjoying it very much indeed, that Jack was fitter than he had been for years, and that they would be delighted, were I ever in that part of the country, to have me as their guest. This suddenly seemed to me the very thing. The Baldwins had never known Charlie Bond, and they would have, therefore, for me no association with his memory. They were jolly, noisy people, with a jolly, noisy family, and Jack Baldwin's personality was so robust that it would surely shake me out of my gloomy mood. I sent a telegram at once to Mrs Baldwin, asking her whether she could have me for a week, and before the day was over I received the warmest of invitations.

Next day I left my fishing village and experienced one of those strange, crooked, in-and-out little journeys that you must undergo if you are to find your way from one obscure Glebeshire village to another.

About midday, a lovely, cold, blue December midday, I discovered myself in Polchester with an hour to wait for my next train. I went down into the town, climbed the High Street to the magnificent cathedral, stood beneath the famous Arden

Gate, looked at the still more famous tomb of the Black Bishop, and it was there, as the sunlight, slanting through the great east window, danced and sparkled about the wonderful blue stone of which that tomb is made, that I had a sudden sense of having been through all this before, of having stood just there in some earlier time, weighed down by some earlier grief, and that nothing that I was experiencing was unexpected. I had a curious sense, too, of comfort and condolence, that horrible grey loneliness that I had felt in the fishing village suddenly fell from me, and for the first time since Bond's death, I was happy. I walked away from the cathedral, down the busy street, and through the dear old market-place, expecting I know not what. All that I knew was that I was intending to go to the Baldwins' and that I would be happy there.

The December afternoon fell quickly, and during the last part of my journey I was travelling in a ridiculous little train, through dusk, and the little train went so slowly and so casually that one was always hearing the murmurs of streams beyond one's window, and lakes of grey water suddenly stretched like plates of glass to thick woods, black as ink, against a faint sky. I got out at my little wayside station, shaped like a rabbit-hutch, and found a motor waiting for me. The drive was not long, and suddenly I was outside the old eighteenth-century house and Baldwin's stout butler was conveying me into the hall with that careful, kindly patronage, rather as though I were a box of eggs that might very easily be broken.

It was a spacious hall, with a large open fireplace, in front of which they were all having tea. I say 'all' advisedly, because the place seemed to be full of people, grown-ups and children, but mostly children. There were so many of these last that I was not, to the end of my stay, to be able to name most of them individually.

Mrs Baldwin came forward to greet me, introduced me to one or two people, sat me down and gave me my tea, told me that I wasn't looking at all well, and needed feeding up, and explained that Jack was out shooting something, but would soon be back.

My entrance had made a brief lull, but immediately everyone recovered and the noise was terrific. There is a lot to be said for the freedom of the modern child. There is a lot to be said against it, too. I soon found that in this party, at any rate, the elders were completely disregarded and of no account. Children rushed about the hall, knocked one another down, shouted and screamed, fell over grown-ups as though they were pieces of furniture, and paid no attention at all to the mild 'Now, children' of a plain, elderly lady who was, I supposed, a governess. I fancy that I was tired with my criss-cross journey, and I soon found a chance to ask Mrs Baldwin if I could go up to my room. She said: 'I expect you find these children noisy. Poor little things. They must have their fun. Jack always says that one can only be young once, and I do so agree with him.'

I wasn't myself feeling very young that evening (I was really about nine hundred years old), so that I agreed with her and eagerly left youth to its own appropriate pleasures. Mrs Baldwin took me up the fine broad staircase. She was a stout, short woman, dressed in bright colours, with what is known, I believe, as an infectious laugh. Tonight, although I was fond of her, and knew very well her good, generous heart, she irritated me, and for some reason that I could not quite define. Perhaps I felt at once that she was out of place there and that the house resented her, but in all this account I am puzzled by the question as to whether I imagine now, on looking back, all sorts of feelings that were not really there at all, but come to me now because

I know of what happened afterwards. But I am so anxious to tell the truth, the whole truth, and nothing but the truth, and there is nothing in the world so difficult to do as that.

We went through a number of dark passages, up and down little pieces of staircase that seemed to have no beginning, no end, and no reason for their existence, and she left me at last in my bedroom, said that she hoped I would be comfortable, and that Jack would come and see me when he came in, and then paused for a moment, looking at me. 'You really don't look well,' she said. 'You've been overdoing it. You're too conscientious. I always said so. You shall have a real rest here. And the children will see that you're not dull.'

Her last two sentences seemed scarcely to go together. I could not tell her about my loss. I realized suddenly, as I had never realized in our older acquaintance, that I should never be able to speak to her about anything that really mattered.

She smiled, laughed and left me. I looked at my room and loved it at once. Broad and low-ceilinged, it contained very little furniture, an old four-poster, charming hangings of some old rose-coloured damask, an old gold mirror, an oak cabinet, some high-backed chairs, and then, for comfort, a large armchair with high elbows, a little quaintly shaped sofa dressed in the same rose colour as the bed, a bright crackling fire and a grandfather clock. The walls, faded primrose, had no pictures, but on one of them, opposite my bed, was a gay sampler worked in bright colours of crimson and yellow and framed in oak.

I liked it, I loved it, and drew the armchair in front of the fire, nestled down into it, and before I knew, I was fast asleep. How long I slept I don't know, but I suddenly woke with a sense of comfort and well-being which was nothing less than exquisite. I belonged to it, that room, as though I had been in it all my days. I had a curious sense of companionship that was exactly what I had been needing during these last weeks. The house was very still, no voices of children came to me, no sound anywhere, save the sharp crackle of the fire and the friendly ticking of the old clock. Suddenly I thought that there was someone in the room with me, a rustle of something that might have been the fire and yet was not.

I got up and looked about me, half-smiling, as though I expected to see a familiar face. There was no one there, of course, and yet I had just that consciousness of companionship that one has when someone whom one loves very dearly and knows very intimately is sitting with one in the same room. I even went to the other side of the four-poster and looked around me, pulled for a moment at the rose-coloured curtains, and of course saw no one. Then the door suddenly opened and Jack Baldwin came in, and I remember having a curious feeling of irritation as though I had been interrupted. His large, breezy, knickerbockered figure filled the room. 'Hullo!' he said, 'delighted to see you. Bit of luck your being down this way. Have you got everything you want?'

II

That was a wonderful old house. I am not going to attempt to describe it, although I have stayed there quite recently. Yes, I stayed there on many occasions since that first of which I am now speaking. It has never been quite the same to me since that first time. You may say, if you like, that the Baldwins fought a battle with it and defeated it. It is certainly now more Baldwin than—well, whatever it was before they rented it. They are not the kind of people to be defeated by atmosphere. Their chief duty in this world, I gather, is to make things Baldwin, and very good for the world too; but when I first went down to them the house was still challenging them. 'A wee bit creepy,' Mrs Baldwin confided to me on the second day of my visit. 'What exactly do you mean by that?' I asked her. 'Ghosts?'

'Oh, there are those, of course,' she answered. 'There's an underground passage, you know, that runs from here to the sea, and one of the wickedest of the smugglers was killed in it, and his ghost still haunts the cellar. At least that's what we were told by our first butler, here; and then, of course, we found that it was the butler, not the smuggler, who was haunting the cellar, and since his departure the smuggler hasn't been visible.' She laughed. All the same, it isn't a comfortable place. I'm going to wake up some of those old rooms. We're going to put in some more windows. And then there are the children,' she added.

Yes, there were the children. Surely the noisiest in all the world. They had reverence for nothing. They were the wildest savages, and especially those from nine to thirteen, the cruellest and most uncivilized age for children. There were two little boys, twins I should think, who were nothing less than devils, and regarded their elders with cold, watching eyes, said nothing in protest when scolded, but evolved plots afterwards that fitted precisely the chastiser. To do my host and hostess justice, all the children were not Baldwin, and I fancy that the Baldwin contingent was the quietest.

Nevertheless, from early morning until ten at night, the noise was terrific and you were never sure how early in the morning it would recommence. I don't know that I personally minded the noise very greatly. It took me out of myself and gave me something better to think of, but, in some obscure and unanalysed way, I felt that the house minded it. One knows how the poets have written about old walls and rafters rejoicing in the happy, careless laughter of children. I do not think this house rejoiced at all, and it was queer how consistently I, who am not supposed to be an imaginative person, thought about the house.

But it was not until my third evening that something really happened. I say 'happened,' but did anything really happen? You shall judge for yourself.

I was sitting in my comfortable armchair in my bedroom, enjoying that delightful half-hour before one dresses for dinner. There was a terrible racket up and down the passages, the children being persuaded, I gathered, to go into the schoolroom and have their supper, when the noise died down and there was nothing but the feathery whisper of the snow—snow had been falling all day—against my window-pane. My thoughts suddenly turned to Bond, directed to him as actually and precipitately as though he had suddenly sprung before me. I did not want to think of him. I had been fighting his memory these last days, because I had thought that the wisest thing to do, but now he was too much for me.

I luxuriated in my memories of him, turning over and over all sorts of times that we had had together, seeing his smile, watching his mouth that turned up at the corners when he was amused, and wondering finally why he should obsess me the way that he did, when I had lost so many other friends for whom I had thought I cared much more, who, nevertheless, never bothered my memory at all. I sighed, and it seemed to me that my sigh was very gently repeated behind me. I turned sharply round. The curtains had not been drawn. You know the strange, milky pallor that reflected snow throws over objects, and although three lighted candles shone in the room, moon-white shadows seemed to hang over the bed and across the floor. Of course there was no one there, and yet I stared and stared about me as though I were convinced that I was not alone. And then I looked especially at one part of the room, a distant corner beyond the four-poster, and it seemed to me that someone was there. And yet no one was there. But whether it was that my mind had been distracted, or that the beauty of the old snow-lit room enchanted me, I don't know, but my thoughts of my friend were happy and reassured. I had not lost him, I seemed to say to myself. Indeed, at that special moment he seemed to be closer to me than he had been while he was alive.

From that evening a curious thing occurred. I only seemed to be close to my friend when I was in my own room—and I felt more than that. When my door was closed and was sitting in my armchair, I fancied that our new companionship was not only Bond's, but was something more as well. I would wake in the middle of the night or in the early morning and feel quite sure that I was not alone; so sure that I did not even want to investigate it further, but just took the companionship for granted and was happy.

Outside that room, however, I felt increasing discomfort. I hated the way in which the house was treated. A quite unreasonable anger rose within me as I heard the Baldwins discussing the improvements that they were going to make, and yet they were so kind to me, and so patently unaware of doing anything that would not generally be commended, it was quite impossible for me to show my anger. Nevertheless, Mrs Baldwin noticed something. 'I am afraid the children are worrying you,' she said one morning, half interrogatively. 'In a way it will be a rest when they go back to school, but the Christmas holidays is their time, isn't it? I do like to see them happy. Poor little dears.'

The poor little dears were at that moment being Red Indians

all over the hall.

'No, of course, I like children,' I answered her. 'The only thing is that they don't—I hope you won't think me foolish—somehow quite fit in with the house.'

'Oh, I think it's so good for old places like this,' said Mrs Baldwin briskly, 'to be woken up a little. I'm sure if the old people who used to live here came back they'd love to hear all the noise and laughter.'

I wasn't so sure myself, but I wouldn't disturb Mrs Baldwin's contentment for anything.

That evening in my room I was so convinced of companionship that I spoke.

'If there's anyone here,' I said aloud, 'I'd like them to know that I'm aware of it and am glad of it.'

Then, when I caught myself speaking aloud, I was suddenly terrified. Was I really going crazy? Wasn't that the first step towards insanity when you talked to yourself? Nevertheless, a moment later I was reassured. There *was* someone there.

That night I woke, looked at my luminous watch and saw that it was a quarter past three. The room was so dark that I could not even distinguish the posts of my bed, but there was a very faint glow from the fire, now nearly dead. Opposite my bed there seemed to me to be something white. Not white in the accepted sense of a tall, ghostly figure; but, sitting up and staring, it seemed to me that the shadow was very small, hardly reaching above the edge of the bed.

'Is there anyone there?' I asked. 'Because, if there is, do speak to me. I'm not frightened. I know that someone has been here all this last week, and I am glad of it.'

Very faintly then, and so faintly that I cannot to this day be sure that I saw anything at all, the figure of a child seemed to me to be visible.

We all know how we have at one time and another fancied that we have seen visions and figures, and then have discovered that it was something in the room, the chance hanging of a coat, the reflection of a glass, a trick of moonlight that has fired our imagination. I was quite prepared for that in this case, but it seemed to me then that as I watched the shadow moved directly in front of the dying fire, and delicate as the leaf of a silver birch, like the trailing rim of some evening clouds, the figure of a child hovered in front of me.

Curiously enough the dress, which seemed to be of some silver tissue, was clearer than anything else. I did not, in fact, see the face at all, and yet I could swear in the morning that I had seen it, that I knew large, black, wide-open eyes, a little mouth very faintly parted in a timid smile, and that, beyond anything else, I had realized in the expression of that face fear and bewilderment and a longing for some comfort.

III

After that night the affair moved very quickly to its little climax.

I am not a very imaginative man, nor have I any sympathy with the modern craze for spooks and spectres. I have never seen, nor fancied that I had seen, anything of a supernatural kind since that visit, but then I have never known since that time such a desperate need of companionship and comfort, and is it not perhaps because we do not want things badly enough in this life that we do not get more of them? However that may be, I was sure on this occasion that I had some companionship that was born of a need greater than mine. I suddenly took the most frantic and unreasonable dislike to the children in that house. It was exactly as though I had discovered somewhere in a deserted part of the building some child who had been left behind by mistake by the last occupants and was terrified by the noisy exuberance and ruthless selfishness of the new family.

For a week I had no more definite manifestation of my little friend, but I was as sure of her presence there in my room as I was of my own clothes and the armchair in which I used to sit.

It was time for me to go back to London, but I could not go. I asked everyone I met as to legends and stories connected with the old house, but I never found anything to do with a little child. I looked forward all day to my hour in my room before dinner, the time when I felt the companionship closest. I sometimes woke in the night and was conscious of its presence, but, as I have said, I never saw anything.

One evening the older children obtained leave to stay up later. It was somebody's birthday. The house seemed to be full of people, and the presence of the children led after dinner to a perfect riot of noise and confusion. We were to play hide-and-seek all over the house. Everybody was to dress up. There was, for that night at least, to be no privacy anywhere. We were all, as Mrs Baldwin said, to be ten years old again. I hadn't the least desire to be ten years old, but I found myself caught into the game, and had, in sheer self-defence, to run up and down the passages and hide behind doors. The noise was terrific. It grew and grew in volume. People got hysterical. The smaller children jumped out of bed and ran about the passages. Somebody kept blowing a motor-horn. Somebody else turned on the gramophone.

Suddenly I was sick of the whole thing, retreated into my room, lit one candle and locked the door. I had scarcely sat down in my chair when I was aware that my little friend had come. She was standing near to the bed, staring at me, terror in her eyes. I have never seen anyone so frightened. Her little breasts panting beneath her silver gown, her very fair hair falling about her shoulders, her little hands clenched. Just as I saw her, there were loud knocks on the door, many voices shouting to be admitted, a perfect babel of noise and laughter. The little figure moved, and then—how can I give any idea of it?—I was conscious of having something to protect and comfort. I saw nothing, physically I felt nothing, and yet I was murmuring, 'There, there, don't mind. They shan't come in. I'll see that no one touches you. I understand. I understand.' For how long I sat like that I don't know. The noises died away, voices murmured at intervals, and then were silent. The house slept. All night I think I stayed there comforting and being comforted.

I fancy now—but how much of it may not be fancy? I knew that the child loved the house, had stayed so long as was possible, at last was driven away, and that that was her farewell, not only to me, but all that she most loved in this world and the next.

I do not know—I could swear to nothing. What I am sure of is that my sense of loss in my friend was removed from that night and never returned. Did I argue with myself that that child companionship included also my friend? Again, I do not know But of one thing I am now sure, that if love is strong enough, physical death cannot destroy it, and however platitudinous that may sound to others, it is platitudinous no longer when you have discovered it by actual experience for yourself.

That moment in that fire-lit room, when I felt that spiritual heart beating with mine, is and always will be enough for me.

One thing more. Next day I left for London, and my wife was delighted to find me so completely recovered—happier, she said, than I had ever been before.

Two days afterwards I received a parcel from Mrs Baldwin.

In the note that accompanied it, she said:

> I think that you must have left this by mistake behind you.
> It was found in the small drawer in your dressing-table.

I opened the parcel and discovered an old blue silk handkerchief, wrapped round a long, thin wooden box. The cover of the box lifted very easily, and I saw inside it an old, painted wooden doll, dressed in the period, I should think, of Queen Anne. The dress was very complete, even down to the little shoes, and the little grey mittens on the hands. Inside the silk skirt there was sewn a little tape, and on the tape, in very faded letters, 'Ann Trelawney, 1710.'

THE TALE OF A CHILD

Josef Bard

Today it is very warm and we shall go and bathe in the Danube. We are not allowed to bathe in the Danube because it is dangerous but we know a spot where there is a bad smell because it is near a factory where they make leather from the hide of oxen. There the water is shallow and we can all stand up in the water. Jacob too can stand up though he is small but he is very wise and Andreas can swim and we all cling to the neck of Roka my dog. Jacob holds most of Roka's neck although Roka is my dog but Jacob is very frightened of the Danube and he would be punished if he drowned, because his father told him so. His father is a man with a curly long black beard and apart from that he is also our grocer and, he has black rings under his eyes. I don't like Jacob's father because he always pats me on the head and then my hair smells of cheese, and I must wash always although I have washed already. But I like Jacob because he is wise. I don't know how but he is very wise. We all play, at marbles after class and we all lose. But Jacob never plays because his father told him so. But he exchanges our bad marbles for better marbles and we buy them from him. Andreas says this is because Jacob is a Jew and his father told him so. I like Andreas but I think he is a liar. He told me the other day there is a dead mason hidden in the walls of every big house. The mason was alive when they walled him in but now he is dead. I don't believe it but I don't like it. Andreas' father is a gentleman who builds houses for others and he told him so.

I am sure Andreas is a liar. Now when we have all come out of the water and were drying ourselves in the grass so that nobody could tell we had been in the Danube and Roka sat down on our clothes and made them wet and we drove Roka away with stones although we all held his neck in the water, now Andreas was chewing a leaf of grass and told us he saw God yesterday early in the afternoon.

'You are a liar,' I said to Andreas. Jacob said nothing but he smiled. He is very wise when he smiles. I saw that Jacob also thought that Andreas was a little liar.

'I am not a liar. I came down to the river and I saw a big white cloud in the sky just like a feather-pillow and God flew out, dipped his feet in the water, smiled at me and flew back again.' So we looked up into they sky. We saw white clouds, fluffy like the sheep in the village and not a bit like feather-pillows. I knew Andreas was a liar. And God simply couldn't fly out of such a cloud.

Still I was envious. I shall be ten years old after two years and I haven't seen God yet. I thought maybe Jacob had more luck. So I asked him: 'Jacob, have you see God?' But Jacob looked frightened and he said he must not speak of God because his father told him so. Then I turned to Andreas again and said to him: 'Andreas, I know you are just lying. Look in my eyes and say again that you saw God!' And Andreas who was lying on his back turned round on his belly and looked at me. Andreas is very beautiful. He has long flaxen locks and his face is very white and his eyes are like brown fruit-drops when you have sucked them and taken them out of your mouth and then hold them in your hand to see how much is left. But I could not look into his eyes as mother looks into mine. His eyes were not in his face they were just like clouds in the sky. So I just said: 'Andreas, I believe you are a liar.' Still I am not quite sure. And then we all went home, Jacob and Andreas and Roka and I and we never said another word.

◆

...today Father eats the marrow-bone. When Father is away I eat the marrow-bone, when he is at home he gives me a bit of the marrow, on a bit of bread, salted and peppered. I was waiting for my bit today but he forgot me. He often is like that. I said: 'Father—' because I am told to call him Father and not Daddie—'Father, Andreas told me he saw God in the afternoon—do you think it is true?' But Father finished the marrow-bone and said I was a donkey. I looked sad and then Mother told Father, 'don't be rude to the child.' Then Father said that Mother spoils me. Then they quarrelled. Then I stopped sulking. I love Mother. All the boys love their Mothers but they respect their Fathers. But my Mother is very beautiful. She has long hair and big eyes and a big mouth and she is soft and plump.

So we were all eating quietly in the garden under the mulberry-tree and the ripe mulberries kept dropping from the tree into my rice-pudding, so wonderful is nature. But still I wanted to know whether Andreas saw God. When Father left the table

I asked Mother: 'Mother dear—do you think Andreas really saw God?' But she looked tired because Father had not kissed her when he left the table because they quarrelled and she sighed. She said: 'The questions you ask! How should I know?' And then she also left the table and followed Father into the house.

Mother is very beautiful and plump but she never answers my questions. I shall ask Kate, our cook who is plumper than Mother but not so very beautiful. She has already told me where babies come from. She will know whether Andreas, the little liar, saw God or not.

◆

...today I have not spoken to Andreas in school because I am not sure whether he is a liar or not. This is a warm morning. The sun is shining and we all wanted to laugh but we had no chance because our teacher Prunk spoke only of serious things and had the birch in his hand. Jacob brought some old stamps and we are all collecting stamps because Jacob says it is the best way to learn the map of the world. Slezak sits behind me and he is the son of our washer-woman, but he hates Jacob. But Slezak is very stupid and our teacher Prunk told him so. We are all a little afraid of Slezak because he is very strong and hits us on the jaw. He says the English all hit each other on the jaw which makes them very strong. Jacob has many English stamps because he has an uncle there who sends them to him. His uncle hits nobody on the jaw but publishes books which others have written, and his father told him so. But when Slezak hit Jacob on the jaw, Jacob smiled mildly and asked him, 'is this what you have learned from your Reverend Father and Jesus Christ?' And Slezak said Jacob crucified Jesus Christ and now he must be hit on the jaw. And we were all very excited and Prunk came in and birched Slezak and told the class we were all Hungarians and we must love each other because anyhow we are only few and our enemies are many. Then he read us a poem which said that the earth is the hat of God and Hungary is a bunch of flowers on the top of the hat. This was written by a great poet called Petöfi, who fell in the battle when the Hungarians were just conquering the Russians. We Hungarians have the habit of winning all the battles but this we lost because we were already tired by conquering the Austrians. The Russians and the Austrians are our enemies and so are others we haven't yet learned about and Prunk says our enemies are many and our friends are few and we must prepare to be proud when the moment arrives when we shall die for Hungary. But we still have time and so we must learn Petöfi's poem by heart and we must not forget that now the Austrians are our friends and our King Francis Joseph rules over them too but he loves only the Hungarians and he only rules over the Austrians because his father told him to. Our King is hanging on the wall and he is very dignified and hairy, and he is now very old but he was young when he began to be a King. When we sing the National Anthem we all look at him and he looks back at us very dignified and hairy.

We all read aloud what is called the poem and it was difficult to remember it because the lines all end the same way, but we were all very proud that we were so few and always conquered our enemies who were many and Slezak wanted to go to the lavatory, which he always wants to do when we must learn something by heart. And Jacob stood up and asked our teacher how could the earth be the hat of God when he told us that the earth was round like a rubber-ball. Jacob is very wise and when we were reading the poem we had quite forgotten that Prunk told us the earth was round.

The Tale of a Child 87

We all looked at Prunk and we all saw clearly he could say just nothing. But he was trying very hard. He said Petőfi was a very great poet and very great poets are permitted to say sometimes what is not quite true. But we all thought that Jacob conquered Prunk. But perhaps Prunk told the truth. And perhaps Andreas is not a little liar but only a great poet?

◆

...today grandma arrived from town. Grandma is a much older lady than Mother but this is only natural. She is small and she always smoothes her mouth with her fingers because her teeth are not natural. But she was sad today because my Uncle Berti came with her who is also her son and Uncle Berti is ill. I don't know what is wrong with Uncle Berti they only say he is mad. I like Uncle Berti because he is so funny, and he sometimes pushes his spoon under his chin because he can't find his mouth and pours the soup under his collar which is a good joke from a grown-up man but Grandma looks sad and kicks me under the table when I laugh. Uncle Berti worked in town and he was almost a bank-director but not quite but this was before he poured the soup under his collar. Now he lives with Grandma who is also his Mother. And he is very big and very silent but he likes to play with me when I play in the garden building castles from mudpies. And Mother and Grandma sat under the mulberry tree and watched us and we sat on the ground and when I turned round I think Mother and Grandma were blowing their noses and I think they wept although Uncle Berti made much better mudpies than I did. And then they went into the house and I followed them to wash my hands and I heard them talk although I did not want to listen but they had not seen me. And Mother was afraid Uncle

Berti would get wild one day and wanted him to go to a place where he could get wild safely. But Grandma only wept and cursed Uncle Berti's wife, but he had two wives and this was unhealthy for him especially when they both loved him. And then I went to the kitchen and just heard Kate the cook say to the maid that Uncle Berti had water in his head but when they saw me they said no more.

And so I went back to Uncle Berti and he was all right doing well with mudpies. And I sat down next to Uncle Berti and looked in his eyes and they were blue but they were not there. And I thought he might perhaps know whether Andreas saw God, so I asked him. And he only said: 'Very-berry-mulberry' and then he smiled. And then he stood up and was very tall and his hair I saw was white and he said, 'let us go to Church I would like to pray.' So I took him by the hand and we went into the house and I said, to Mother 'Uncle Berti and I want to go to Church.' And Mother looked frightened but Grandma said it was all right. And so we walked out, I holding his hand and I took him to the chapel although it was three o'clock in the afternoon and God is seldom at home at that hour. And it was very dark and cool in the chapel and candles burnt in the corners and I was not comfortable because Uncle Berti held my hand very tight. And I don't go to Church because Father says he hates all the priests and if there is God there is only one who also hates the priests. But it is beautiful in our chapel it smells good not like near the river where they make leather from the hide of oxen. And the lady-saints were very beautiful and they all had flowers on the altar. We just stood in the middle of the chapel and we were quite alone and it was very silent. And Uncle Berti whispered into my ear whether I could see a gentleman-saint because he would like to pray before a gentleman-saint and not before a lady-saint today. And I found his one in the right corner who was tied to a tree and he was very naked but there were arrows in him. And Uncle Berti let my hand go and fell on his knees and began to pray, but it seemed to have little sense and I wondered whether the saint would understand what he was saying. Then Uncle Berti wept and he wept very loud and I was afraid because it was very silent and we were alone and I had heard Mother say Uncle Berti might get wild. But it was not true because he stood up and was very quiet and stroked my hand and thanked me for taking him to the chapel. It was all right what he said, so I told him why did he let himself be called mad. Then he laughed and he laughed just as loud as he wept before, and I got frightened again. But he became quiet again and we walked out of the chapel and he said he wanted to buy me something. So I took him to Jacob's father who is the grocer and I chose a box of green lizards made of rubber-candy. And Jacob's father made big eyes and forgot to pat me on the head which made me grateful. And Uncle Berti shook hands with Jacob's father and forgot to pay and we all went back to Mother and Grandma.

Then Grandma and Uncle Berti went to the station and we accompanied them and Uncle Berti was so big and Grandma very small but she led him by the hand. And Uncle Berti was very pale and when he shook hands with me, my heart hurt because I was now sorry for him. I wished he had something better than water in his head.

◆

...today we went to swim in the Danube again where it stinks but it is safe and I kept my head out of water because I was afraid water might get into my head through my ears as with Uncle Berti. We are friends again with Andreas and I always like Jacob because he is wise. And we went rather late and we rolled about naked and Jacob was different because he was taken into the bosom of Abraham that way and it happened when he was eight days old and his father told him so. Jacob has very thin legs and thin arms and Andreas is much more beautiful but Andreas rolled very close to me and I told him I didn't like it because we must only love girls and Kate the cook told me so. And so Andreas rolled on his belly and his bottom was turned towards me and it seemed beautiful but it was his bottom and bottoms are ugly because my Mother told me so and you must never show it except when you are alone and the doctor asks you to. I told this to Andreas but he laughed and then he lied again because he must always lie except when he is a great poet. Andreas lied that children are made of marble and rose-leaves and they are beautiful everywhere and we only cover our bottoms because otherwise we would be too beautiful for our parents. So I called him a liar because I know babies are made by mothers and Slezak the son of our washer-woman brought me the cord which came out with him into the world and he found it in a drawer and it was wrapped in a paper and it was brown and horrid. And Jacob said we must not bother about this, but collect stamps in peace and learn the map of the world because his father told him so.

But I still called Andreas a liar because I saw our dog Roka starting to make babies to his wife and Kate the cook told me father was not different. Andreas did not answer but smelt the daisies in the grass. Then he said he didn't care what we knew but he dreamt babies were made of marbles and rose-leaves. Now I knew he was lying again because I dreamt that uncle Berti came back and I broke a hole in his head with my hatchet and all the water flowed out and our teacher Prunk was drowned in the flood but it was not true because in the morning I saw that Prunk was still alive and teaching history. I wanted Jacob to be on my side against Andreas but Jacob is very wise and he only wants to collect stamps in peace.

So I teased Andreas who was still smelling the daisies which I know have no smell and told him if he knew everything did he know what the stars were. Andreas said he knew but he couldn't say it because he didn't know the words. So I asked him did he know what the moon was. And Andreas said the moon is a pale woman who is looking for a lost world. And then I got frightened just like in the chapel when uncle Berti wept aloud and I thought perhaps water had got into the ears of Andreas because I also see ghosts in the dark but I know they are not there because my Mother told me so. So I asked him what the sun is and Andreas lifted his head and said the sun is an angry flame which wants to burn everything and the earth is running away from him because he is frightened. And Jacob and I were also frightened and it was now dark and Jacob said we must not ask more questions from Andreas because he is perhaps a prophet and we must be happy when prophets are silent because his father told him so. And we all walked home and said no more.

◆

...today I saw Kate the cook drinking rum in the kitchen but I shall not tell Mother because Kate is my friend and always answers my questions and Mother is more beautiful but she never answers my questions and Father is always angry. And Kate gave some rum to Peti the milkman who always smells of what the cows leave when they don't behave properly and who is waiting on the cows. And Peti the milkman started to be like Roka my dog when he joined his wife but Kate pushed him back and asked him whether he was not ashamed before the child which was me. And then I remembered that Lola had her birthday and she had asked me to come and have some of her birthday cake and I had not asked Mother because now it was after dinner and I had to go to bed. So I asked Kate to let me in through the kitchen door when I came back and then I went into the garden and picked white and red roses which she liked and walked to Lola's house because I think I love Lola and I would like to marry Lola if she could preserve herself till I grow up. Because Lola is already very big and her hair is perfumed when she kisses me and she lives in a big house, with a big orchard where a brook flows through and she has many young men playing the piano with her which is very musical. And when I arrived she was playing but she stopped and kissed me again and her hair was again perfumed. And there were many people and they were eating sandwiches and Lola wore a long white dress and her arms were puffed but this was only her dress and not her arms. And everybody was very nice to me though they laughed and a fat man who played with Lola pinched my cheeks, and I told him I didn't like that and I thought he was stupid. I said this because I saw him breathe down on Lola's neck when she played the piano and I love Lola. And Lola saw that I was angry and she said we two will go out into the garden, and so we went out and we sat down under a cherry tree and we sat on the grass and I put my head on Lola's white neck and kissed it which Lola said I must not do. And Lola was sad and she looked up at the moon and she sighed. And she said, 'Do you see the moon?' And I said, 'Yes, I see the moon she is like a pale woman looking for a lost world.'

The Tale of a Child 93

And then I blushed because I remembered that I had heard this from Andreas, that little liar. But Lola did not remember it and she kissed me on the mouth and said that it was very beautiful and asked me whether I could say something else as beautiful. Then I said the sun is an angry flame which wants to burn everything and the earth is running away from him because he is frightened. Then I blushed again because I remembered that I heard this also from Andreas the little liar. But Lola kissed me on the mouth again and she said how poetic children are and I saw she thought of the fat man who was not so poetic and then she said I must come when I had something beautiful to say and that she would always kiss me. So we parted in the garden and I did not go back to the house with her because I didn't like the fat man but Lola went back and I walked to my home. I was very happy and wondered what the stars were but then Father was waiting for me in the kitchen and he said he would break my bones if I left the house without permission at night and he began doing so, but Mother came and told him not to be rude to the child and then they quarrelled and I hurried to my room before they had finished and I thought I hated to be beaten and I would kill whoever dares to beat me, only fathers unfortunately can't be killed because my Mother told me so. So I went to bed and I dreamt of Lola but it was not true because I could not remember it in the morning.

◆

...today Slezak was late for school because he said his mother had borne him a brother which is curious because Slezak has no father. But we did not ask questions because Prunk told us more about our history and he said we Hungarians were somewhere else a thousand years ago and we had the habit of multiplying ourselves quickly so we went out to find another home so we came to Hungary which is where we now are and we conquered the people we found here because we had the habit of winning all the battles. But it was not easy to find Hungary because it was far from the place where we multiplied ourselves, but our very own Battle-god sent us a bird and he flew ahead of us and when we arrived he flew back to our very own Battle-god and so Prunk said we have been in Hungary now for over a thousand years and had much glory and we have fought against the Turks who also belonged to our enemies but we haven't yet learnt about them and we have suffered much glory because we were only few and our enemies were many. And we were all very proud but then Jacob stood up and asked Prunk why we had so many enemies. Prunk knows much and has a big wart on his forehead but Jacob is wise and Prunk thought a little while and then said we are the bunch of flowers on God's hat and our neighbours are all envious of us. Then we all stood up and sang the National Anthem and our King Francis Joseph hanging on the wall listened to us and he listened to our promise that we would all die here because we couldn't go elsewhere. Then Prunk left us for half an hour to give us time to wash our hands and eat our bread and butter and we all stood round Slezak who was sad because now his mother can't wash for a month and he did not want a brother because they are very poor and his father died when they hit him on the head with a bottle of rum. Slezak said it was Peti the milkman who did it to his mother but he would buy a gun and shoot him. Then Andreas pulled me by the sleeve and we all left Slezak and whispered because Andreas asked us to collect money for Slezak because he is very poor. And we all promised to give him our pocket money for the week and to ask our parents to give him money. Then Slezak had to go to

Prunk's room and he came back weeping because Prunk asked him to leave the school. And we all hated Prunk and called him an ugly wart which he had on his forehead. And when Prunk came back to teach history we all stood up and Jacob walked in front of us and asked Prunk in the name of the class to take back Slezak because Slezak is innocent because he did not tell Peti the milkman to do it to his mother. Then Prunk was very angry and told Jacob to go back to his place and said we should not know about such things and that Slezak was a bad influence. Then he taught us more about our glorious past and how we conquered our enemies and how our Kings helped us but I don't remember because we did not listen because we thought of Slezak. And when the class was over Prunk saw that we were all sad and he said he would talk about Slezak to the headmaster. Then we all cheered and were proud again of our glorious past.

◆

...today is Friday evening and I was permitted to go to Jacob's house and have dinner with them because I gave some old stamps to Jacob and he was grateful. And it was very warm in the room and we all kept our hats on our heads because Jacob's God likes that and also we were more than thirteen because otherwise Jacob's God is not present. And Jacob's father was very clean and he had a white stole on his neck and he prayed loud and we all murmured and then we had soup with big dumplings in it and we had roast goose with much stuffings. And Jacob's relatives were there and they had beards but the women were only fat. Jacob has no mother but his aunt cooks for him and she is called Hannah and she is only half-witted but she cooks well. Jacob says Jews are wise, but when they are not they are very stupid. It was very hot and we were not happy because

Jacob's God really lives in Palestine and only comes for a short visit to our village. And I said to Jacob now we will go to my garden and eat fruit from the trees.

And then we walked home which is not far because our village is small. And Jacob was sad because he had no mother and Friday night he always remembers her. So I told him stories to amuse him how the Austrian villagers carry ladders sideways through the forest and cut down the trees to make way. But Jacob was still sad and I looked up at the stars and wondered what they were and whether Andreas the little liar had found the words for them. Then I told Jacob about Lola and that I was, going to marry her if she can preserve herself until I grow up but Jacob only smiled and he said I would forget her when I grew up. I know Jacob is very wise but I don't believe what he said. But when we turned into my garden we could not eat fruit because we found Kate the cook weeping under the mulberry tree and Father came out and told her she must go away, because she wanted to push the carving knife into Peti the milkman because Peti did it to Slezak's mother and he also did it to Kate, and Peti also had a wife. Peti must be very healthy because now he has three wives and has no water in his head and uncle Berti had only two wives and his head was full of water. But Mother came out and she is very kind and she patted Kate on the cheek and told her to stay and she sent Father back into the house. And then a policeman came because Kate had just scratched Peti with the carving knife and the policeman wanted Kate to go with him but Father said everything was all right and gave a cigar to the policeman and then Peti came with his head bandaged and said it was all a misunderstanding and Kate remained with us but we shall get milk elsewhere. And Father said to Peti that he would break his bones if he ever dared to come to our house again but Mother said don't be rude to the poor fellow and sent Father into the house. Then Kate went to bed weeping and Peti and the policeman left and I took Jacob to the garden gate because it was now late. And Jacob who is so wise said to me it is much better to collect stamps in peace. He said love is very unhappy always because his father told him so.

◆

...today when Father was eating my marrow-bone I asked him to give me money because we are collecting for Slezak in school. But Father said he had no money to throw away and I looked sad and Mother said to Father don't be rude to the child. And then they quarrelled. And when we were left alone under the mulberry-tree, Mother said she would give me money but I must be nicer to Father. And I said I am very nice to him but he never talks to me. Mother said Father works for us and he is tired and we must cheer him up. All fathers must be cheered up. They all work for their wives and children and when they don't they are not happy. So I must not forget to greet Father when I see him in the morning which I always do. So I asked Mother why she married Father and she said the questions children ask and left me alone. Mother is plump and beautiful but I don't understand her. I understand Kate much better who is now very plump. But I love Mother and she gave me money for Slezak. Slezak is now back in school with us and he wanted to give me his cord which is in a tissue paper because he is grateful because I collected for him but I did not want his cord because it is horrid. Slezak is very stupid and he hit Jacob on the jaw because he said it will make him strong because the English all hit each other on the jaw which makes them strong. But Jacob always says he hates violence because his father told him so.

Slezak is also very happy because the brother his mother bore him recently died yesterday and now Slezak is again his mother's only orphan. And he asked us to come and see him because he is now in a coffin over the washing-tub and candles burn. And in the afternoon we all went to see Slezak's brother, Jacob and Andreas and Roka and I but Roka had to wait outside in the courtyard. And Slezak's brother was in a small white coffin and Slezak's mother who is our washer-woman when she has no babies gave rum to her friends who came to see her and she wanted to give rum to us too but we did not want it. So we just stared at the candles and we were silent and Jacob was sad because he remembered his mother as on Friday evenings and Andreas was very pale and he whispered something but I could not hear it. Then we all coughed because we wanted to go out and Slezak's mother thanked us for coming and thanked us for collecting money for Slezak who is only a silly bully. Then she wept and her cheeks were all very red like apples and when she wiped her tears I saw her hands were all red from washing. So we coughed again and blew our noses and went out into the courtyard because the room opens on a courtyard which is not clean. And Roka was chewing an old bone which he had found on the dustheap and we took it away from him. But Slezak only stood there leaning against the door and he looked on the ground and he forgot to hit Jacob on the jaw to make him strong which he always does.

◆

...today we are very excited because Aunt Leonie arrived who is also my Mother's sister. And she married an Austrian who lives in Vienna where also lives our King Francis Joseph when he rules over the Austrians. But Aunt Leonie married long ago and now she has children and she brought one called Pamperl which sounds silly but is Austrian because the Viennese are also Austrian. Aunt Leonie married Uncle Pepi because he was beautiful and he sang songs about Vienna which is also beautiful and he was very funny and because she thought Uncle Pepi was almost a bank-director but he was only a great traveller for business and he always was travelling when Aunt Leonie had the babies. So we all sat under the mulberry-tree and Aunt Leonie wept and she had anyhow watery eyes and Father said why did she marry Uncle Pepi and she must go back to Uncle Pepi because now they had four children and then Aunt Leonie finished her cake and wept some more and Mother said to Father don't be rude to my sister and then we were left alone.

Then Mother asked Aunt Leonie what she intended to do and Aunt Leonie said the children should go for a walk. And I took Pamperl by the hand which is very soft and we walked out and Pamperl who has a sallow face and a lace collar talked to me but it was Austrian or Viennese and it sounded funny but I could not understand it. So we walked to the river and I led Pamperl through the dam where the water is very wild and I thought it was a pity the Austrians were our friends now and our King Francis Joseph rules over them also, because otherwise I would push Pamperl into the water and then Uncle Pepi and Aunt Leonie would have only three children and we would all be happier. But I hurried through the dam and I took Pamperl to where we bathe and I wanted Pamperl to bathe in the river because I thought Pamperl might drown without my help and then we should have one enemy less when the Austrians will be our enemies again, because we are only few and our enemies are many. But Pamperl shrieked and so I walked back with him to our house. And there we found Uncle Pepi who is very bald but has a lovely beard and a moustache like our King Francis Joseph but he is not so dignified because he always laughs. And Uncle Pepi followed my Aunt from Vienna because he thought now that he loved her better than Gullash and beer which he loves very much. And he took Pamperl on his knees and gave him beer and he sang a song about a Viennese cab which all Viennese sing and is also loved by our King Francis Joseph when he rules over the Austrians. Mother was sad and told Aunt Leonie that she must go back to Vienna tomorrow. And we went to bed but I slept only little because Uncle Pepi sang about the Viennese cab all night long.

◆

...today Slezak hit the butcher's son on the jaw who called him a bastard and then Slezak hit him again and Jacob asked Slezak whether he had learnt this from his Reverend Father and Jesus Christ our Saviour because Jacob hates violence and wants us all to collect stamps in peace. Slezak hit Jacob on the jaw but only to make him strong. But I stood up for Slezak because he was called a bastard which was true but not very beautiful. And Slezak wanted to give me his cord again but I did not want it because it is horrid. Then he wanted to give me holy pictures which he got from our Reverend Father because Slezak has very good marks in religion and the Reverend Father calls him a lost sheep who is now back with the flock. And the holy picture was very beautiful and the Virgin Mary on it looked like Lola whom I love only Lola has no baby. But I did not take the holy picture because if there is a God there is only one who hates the priests because my Father told me so. Then Slezak who is very grateful because I have also collected money for him said he would tell me a secret but I must swear not to tell it to anybody else. And he told me there is a house in our village which stands alone in a meadow and which is always shut with green shutters during the day because the ladies who live there always sleep during the day and only wake up at night. And they are all very beautiful because they are all painted and perfumed and he knows one lady called Amanta who looks like the Virgin Mary on the picture only she is not a virgin although she has no baby. And they have many visitors during the night but they are all men who want no babies. And I thought Slezak was lying to me and I told him so but Slezak swore it was all true because his mother is washing for the ladies who sleep during the day and it is all very beautiful and full of mirrors and he went one day with his mother to help with the laundry and his mother told him not to look but he looked very much. And now I remembered I had seen the house with the green shutters alone in the meadow but I did not know ladies lived there who were sleeping during the day just like in the fairytales. So when I went home from school I asked mother to come with me for a walk and she was happy because I always go with Jacob and Andreas. And then I wanted to go where the house with the green shutters stood and we saw it standing alone in the meadow. I told Mother to look what a beautiful house it was. But she blushed and said it was an ugly house and I must never go near it. And I said I thought it was the house of the Sleeping Beauty which I read in the tales. But Mother said this was a very bad house and I must promise never to go near it. Mother is plump and very beautiful but she never answers my questions. Kate the cook always answers them. So I went to the kitchen to ask Kate about the fairy castle which stands alone in the meadow because I also dreamt of the fairies but I can't remember. But Peti the milkman was there although my Father will break his bones because he told him so. Peti still smells of cows but Kate our cook loves him again. He also gave me a whistle which he brought for me but I will wash it because Peti made it wet with his mouth. And Kate is now very plump and she weeps but she says she loves Peti again because the baby died which Peti did to Slezak's mother and Peti's wife has also the dry rot and she will die soon and then Peti will marry Kate. And we were all very happy and Kate gave him goose-liver. And I wanted to ask Kate about the house but I thought she would not know because she is only a cook and she cooks well but she never told me a good fairy-tale. I think I shall not ask anyone about the house standing alone in the meadow because all the people I know sleep during the night and they would know nothing about the ladies who sleep during the day.

◆

...today it is almost summer and now we know already how to add up and subtract and multiply and divide and we have learnt about most of our enemies and of our glorious past and how the Austrians have always swindled us after we have so often conquered them. And we have learned many poems and I think Petöfi wrote better poems than the one about God's hat and I have learned some and I have won a prize for reading poetry. And now we sing the anthem in tune to our King who hangs on the wall. And soon school will be over and then Mother and I shall go to the Lake Balaton which is the most beautiful lake in the world where all the Hungarians go and the Jewish Hungarians live on one end and the Roman Catholic Hungarians on the other and scattered in between are the rest. But I am

The Tale of a Child 103

not very happy because Lola whom I love will marry the fat man whom I hate and she will kiss the fat man with the same mouth with which she kissed me and she will not wait for me and preserve herself. And I am sad because Grandma came and told us that Uncle Berti is now very wild and he wants to eat his collar-buttons with his breakfast and he will die because now he has more water in his head. So I went out with Roka and looked for Jacob and then we went to find Andreas to ask him to bathe with us in the Danube. Andreas lives in a big house called a villa and he sat in the garden with his mother who has very soft hands which I like. So we kissed her hands and Roka misbehaved on the flowers and we asked Andreas to come with us. And Andreas was reading a book of poems by a poet called Shelley who was also loved by our poet Petöfi. Andreas got the book today because he only wants to read poetry and he said Shelley died very young and he was English but very frail, but that was perhaps because they did not hit him on the jaw to make him strong. And the father of Andreas came out into the garden and smiled at us because he is very kind and he builds houses for others and when you do that you can build some for yourself. So we all went to the Danube where it smells but it is safe and we went into the water holding Roka's neck. And I said the Danube was very beautiful this afternoon because the water was blue and green and when the leather did not stink the acacia-trees smelt sweet on the banks. But Andreas says the Danube is not very beautiful and the people who love along the Danube are all very unhappy. Andreas has travelled much already because his father takes him along with him and he has seen high mountains and he told us stories 'of beautiful lakes in Italy'. So I was sad that the Danube was not very beautiful and we scampered back to the riverside to dry in the grass and

I told Andreas to move away because we must love only girls because Kate the cook told me so. And Jacob was also very sad because his father has a bad heart and that is why he has rings under his eyes and I thought of Lola who was not faithful to me. And we all ate grass and lay on our bellies and I said when we grow up we shall also have rings under our eyes and bad hearts and perhaps water in our heads like uncle Berti and how nice it would be to preserve ourselves. And Andreas rolled on his back and looked into the clouds which were swimming over the sky and he said everything passes away only the clouds pass and stay and I thought this was very beautiful and I could easily have told it to Lola and she would have kissed me on the mouth but now she has married the fat man who is not so poetic as we are. And I also thought this Danube river comes from Vienna where Uncle Pepi and Pamperl live and where our King Francis Joseph enjoys to hear the song of Uncle Pepi. But I got tired of thinking and I played with Roka who rolled on his back and watched Andreas who always looks into the clouds when he finds some in the sky, and I asked Andreas whether he had seen God fly out again because perhaps he said the truth after all and Andreas said he wanted to fly with the wind and hold the whole world against his heart. And he said he hated to think that one day he must die and he said there were many Gods and most of them hated us and that is why we must die. But Jacob who is very wise said that he must not say such things and there is only one God who punishes those who call him names and we must all collect stamps in peace and learn the map of the world, because his father told him so. But Andreas was not listening to him because he still watched the clouds swimming in the blue sky and I pinched him to wake him up and then he rose and we all walked home very silent and said no more.

DUSK

'Saki' (H.H. Munro)

Norman Gortsby sat on a bench in the Park, with his back to a strip of bush-planted sward, fenced by the park railings, and the Row fronting him across a wide stretch of carriage drive. Hyde Park Corner, with its rattle and hoot of traffic, lay immediately to his right. It was some thirty minutes past six on an early March evening, and dusk had fallen heavily over the scene, dusk mitigated by some faint moonlight and many street lamps. There was a wide emptiness over road and sidewalk, and yet there were many unconsidered figures moving silently through the half-light or dotted unobtrusively on bench and chair, scarcely to be distinguished from the shadowed gloom in which they sat. The scene pleased Gortsby and harmonized with his present mood. Dusk, to his mind, was the hour of the defeated. Men and women, who had fought and lost, who hid their fallen fortunes and dead hopes as far as possible from the scrutiny of the curious, came forth in this hour of gloaming, when their shabby clothes and bowed shoulders and unhappy eyes might pass unnoticed, or, at any rate, unrecognized.

A king that is conquered must see strange looks,
So bitter a thing is the heart of man.

The wanderers in the dusk did not choose to have strange looks fasten on them, therefore they came out in this bat-fashion, taking their pleasure sadly in a pleasure-ground that had emptied of its rightful occupants. Beyond the sheltering screen of bushes and palings came a realm of brilliant lights and noisy, rushing traffic. A blazing, many-tiered stretch of windows shone through the dusk and almost dispersed it, marking the haunts of those other people, who held their own in life's struggle, or at any rate had not had to admit failure. So Gortsby's imagination pictured things as he sat on his bench in the almost deserted walk. He was in the mood to count himself among the defeated. Money troubles did not press on him; had he so wished he could have strolled into the thoroughfares of light and noise, and taken his place among the jostling ranks of those who enjoyed prosperity or struggled for it. He had failed in a more subtle ambition, and for the moment he was heart sore and disillusioned, and not disinclined to take a certain cynical pleasure in observing and labeling his fellow wanderers as they went their ways in the dark stretches between the lamp-lights.

On the bench by his side sat an elderly gentleman with a drooping air of defiance that was probably the remaining vestige of self-respect in an individual who had ceased to defy successfully anybody or anything. His clothes could scarcely be called shabby, at least they passed muster in the half-light, but one's imagination could not have pictured the wearer embarking on the purchase of a half-crown box of chocolates or laying out ninepence on a carnation buttonhole. He belonged unmistakably to that forlorn orchestra to whose piping no one dances; he was one of the world's lamenters who induces no responsive weeping. As he rose to go Gortsby imagined him returning to a home circle where he was snubbed and of no account, or to some bleak lodging where his ability to pay a weekly bill was the beginning and end of the interest he inspired. His retreating figure vanished slowly into the shadows, and his place on the bench was taken almost immediately by a young man, fairly well-dressed but scarcely more cheerful of mein than his predecessor. As if to emphasize the fact that the world went badly with him the newcomer unburdened himself of an angry and very audible expletive as he flung himself into the seat.

'You don't seem in a very good temper,' said Gortsby, judging that he was expected to take due notice of the demonstration.

The young man turned to him with a look of disarming frankness which put him instantly on his guard.

'You wouldn't be in a good temper if you were in the fix I'm in,' he said; 'I've done the silliest thing I've ever done in my life.'

'Yes?' said Gortsby dispassionately.

'Came up this afternoon, meaning to stay at the Patagonian Hotel in Berkshire Square,' continued the young man; 'when I got there I found that it had been pulled down some weeks ago and a cinema theatre run up on the site. The taxi driver recommended me to another hotel some way off and I went there. I just sent a letter to my people, giving them the address, and then I went out to buy some soap—I'd forgotten to pack any and I hate using hotel soap. Then I strolled about a bit, had a drink at a bar and looked at the shops, and when I came to turn my steps back to the hotel I suddenly realized that I didn't remember its name or even what street it was in. There's a nice predicament for a fellow who hasn't any friends or connections in London! Of course I can wire to my people for the address, but they won't have got my letter till tomorrow; meantime I'm without any money, came out with about a shilling on me, which went in buying the soap and getting the drink, and here I am, wandering about with two pence in my pocket and nowhere to go for the night.'

'There was an eloquent pause after the story had been told. I suppose you think I've spun you rather an impossible yarn,' said the young man presently, with a suggestion of resentment in his voice.

'Not at all impossible,' said Gortsby judicially; 'I remember doing exactly the same thing once in a foreign capital, and on that occasion there were two of us, which made it more remarkable. Luckily we remembered that the hotel was on a sort of canal, and when we struck the canal we were able to find our way back to the hotel.'

The youth brightened at the reminiscence. 'In a foreign city I wouldn't mind so much,' he said; 'one could go to one's Consul and get the requisite help from him. Here in one's own land one is far more derelict if one gets into a fix. Unless I can find some decent chap to swallow my story and lend me some money I seem likely to spend the night on the Embankment. I'm glad, anyhow, that you don't think the story outrageously improbable.'

He threw a good deal of warmth into the last remark, as though perhaps to indicate his hope that Gortsby did not fall far short of the requisite decency.

'Of course,' said Gortsby slowly, 'the weak point of your story is that you can't produce the soap.'

The young man sat forward hurriedly, felt rapidly in the

pockets of his overcoat, and then jumped to his feet.

'I must have lost it,' he muttered angrily.

'To lose an hotel and a cake of soap on one afternoon suggests wilful carelessness,' said Gortsby, but the young man scarcely waited to hear the end of the remark. He flitted away down the path, his head held high, with an air of somewhat jaded jauntiness.

'It was a pity,' mused Gortsby; 'the going out to get one's own soap was the one convincing touch in the whole story, and yet it was just that little detail that brought him to grief. If he had had the brilliant forethought to provide himself with a cake of soap, wrapped and sealed with all the solicitude of the chemist's counter, he would have been a genius in his particular line. In his particular line genius certainly consists of an infinite capacity for taking precautions.'

With that reflection Gortsby rose to go; as he did so an exclamation of concern escaped him. Lying on the ground by the side of the bench was a small oval packet, wrapped and sealed with the solicitude of a chemist's counter. It could be nothing else but a cake of soap, and it had evidently fallen out of the youth's overcoat pocket when he flung himself down on the seat. In another moment Gortsby was scudding along the dusk-shrouded path in anxious quest for a youthful figure in a light overcoat. He had nearly given up the search when he caught sight of the object of his pursuit standing irresolutely on the border of the carriage drive, evidently uncertain whether to strike across the Park or make for the bustling pavements of Knightsbridge. He turned round sharply with an air of defensive hostility when he found Gortsby hailing him.

'The important witness to the genuineness of your story has turned up,' said Gortsby, holding out the cake of soap; 'it must have slid out of your overcoat pocket when you sat down on the seat. I saw it on the ground after you left. You must excuse my disbelief, but appearances were really rather against you, and now, as I appealed to the testimony of the soap, I think I ought to abide by its verdict. If the loan of a sovereign is any good to you—'

The young man hastily removed all doubt on the subject by pocketing the coin.

'Here is my card with my address,' continued Gortsby; 'any day this week will do for returning the money, and here is the soap—don't lose it again; it's been a good friend to you.'

'Lucky thing your finding it,' said the youth, and then, with a catch in his voice, he blurted out a word or two of thanks and fled headlong in the direction of Knightsbridge.

'Poor boy, he is as nearly as possible broke down,' said Gortsby to himself. 'I don't wonder either; the relief from his quandary must have been acute. It's a lesson to me not to be too clever in judging by circumstances.'

As Gortsby retraced his steps past the seat where the little drama had taken place he saw an elderly gentleman poking and peering beneath it and on all sides of it, and recognized his earlier fellow occupant.

'Have you lost anything, sir?' he asked.

'Yes, sir, a cake of soap.'

BOY AMONG THE WRITERS

David Garnett

Joseph Conrad paid many visits to the Cearne. On one of the first occasions, when I was five years old, I asked him why the first mate of a ship was always a bad man and the second mate good. I don't know what stories I had been reading which had put this into my head, but I remember Conrad's laughing and confusing me by saying: 'For many years I was a first mate myself.'

It was next morning that we made friends. There was a jolly wind, and it was washing day. I was alone with Conrad, and suddenly he was making me a sailing boat. The sail was a clean sheet tied at the top corners to a clothes-prop and hoisted with some spare clothesline over one of the clothes-posts. The sail was lashed at the foot, and I held the sheet fastened to the other corner in one hand while it bellied and pulled. The green grass heaved in waves, the sail filled and tugged, our speed was terrific. Alterations were made and the rig perfected and when, an hour later, Edward[1] came out looking for his guest, he found him sitting in our big clothes basket steering the boat and giving me orders to take in or let out the sail.

I met Conrad again when my mother and I were staying with Ford and Elsie Hueffer at Aldington knoll, a little Kentish farmhouse looking out over Romney Marsh. Ford was at his most lovable and genial. There was a stream running through the garden, and Ford had installed a little wooden water-wheel with two brightly-painted wooden puppets who seemed to be working very hard as they bent down and straightened up incessantly. Really the water turned the wheel and the wheel made them move up and down, bending their backs.

He later adopted the name of Ford Madox Ford, and some people regard him as a great novelist. At the time I first remember him, Ford was a very young man, tall and Germanic in appearance, with a pink and white complexion, pale, rather prominent, blue eyes and a beard which I referred to, when we first met, as 'hay on his face', in spite of the fact that I had been well-broken into beards by those of Sergey Stepniak and Peter Kropotkin.

Ford married Elsie Martindale, whom he first met at school when they were both small children. Elsie was tall, high-breasted and dark, with a bold eye and a rich, high colour, like a ripe nectarine. She dressed in richly-coloured garments of the William Morris style and wore earrings and a great amber necklace, and I, at the age of five, was at once greatly attracted by her. Without undue hesitation I proposed marriage, and when Elsie pointed out that Ford was an obstacle, I said cheerfully

---

[1] Edward Garnett, the author's father, most gifted of publisher's advisers; his occupation, 'the discovery of talent in unknown writers.'

that it would be a good thing if he died soon. Although Ford was at once informed of my intention of superseding him, he bore no rancor and was a most charming entertainer of my youth. He would suddenly squat and then bound after me like a gigantic frog. He could twitch one ear without moving the other—dreadful but fascinating accomplishment. He would also tell me stories, just as he told everyone else stories—but I do not think I ever believed that anything he said was true.

The next time we saw the Hueffers they had moved from Aldington Knoll to Winchelsea, and we stayed in lodgings next door to them. The South African War was drawing to a close; it was perhaps the late summer of 1901. There was a flower show in Winchelsea the day after we arrived, and troops paraded in dark green uniforms with felt hats turned up on one side, and the military band played 'The Last Rose of Summer' and other airs through a long, hot and dusty afternoon. I had been given a Brownie Kodak. A few days later we went over in a hired wagonette to Rye and called upon Henry James, whom we found dressed in an extremely tight-fitting pair of knickerbockers and an equally exiguous jacket of black-and-white checks. When he came out with us and showed us Rye he wore a very tight-fitting cap on his vast head. In this costume he was kind enough to pose for me, and the photograph I took came out perfectly. Lamb House astonished me by its tidiness, the beautiful furniture in the drawing-room, the perfection of a passage and the beautiful garden. Ford, tall and fresh-coloured, smiling and showing his rabbit teeth, enjoyed himself, patronizing my parents on one side and James on the other. Perhaps my parents were aware of the possibility that they were being thrust upon the Master by Ford. If they were right in that suspicion! I am duly grateful to Ford, for I should not otherwise have had tea with Henry

James in Lamb House. He walked back a little way with us, and we said goodbye to him on the edge of Rye and walked down from the high ground to where our conveyance was waiting.

Then a new visitor came to the Cearne to win my heart. He was W.H. Hudson, a very tall lean man with red-brown eyes which could flare up with anger or amusement and then die down again. He had a short beard, a twisted aquiline nose that had been broken in some fight in South America, a wide forehead and a curiously flat top to his head, and big bony hands. His voice, gentle and deep in tone, became suddenly rasping and fierce when Edward teased him—which he was always doing. Hudson wore an old-fashioned tail-coat made of some pepper-and-salt or brown tweed with pockets in the tails and a stand-up, stiff white collar to his shirt.

His first visit was in winter, but he came again in the spring and summer following. One spring morning I went out with him into the woods; the majority of the trees were still bare; only the hawthorn and a few forward sprays of beech were covered with leaves. I was astonished because he continually identified birds by their song, and the song of a missel-thrush led us to a missel-thrush's nest in the fork of a young oak. Standing silently in the warm spring sunshine, listening to the wild and rapturous song of the storm-cock, I felt very close to my tall companion.

I told him that I had seen a frog unlike other frogs. Together we went down across the fields below the Cearne to Trevereux pond where there was a nightingale singing, and there Hudson found my 'other frog' which was in reality a kind of toad—a natterjack.

Hudson's next visit was in the summer. It was a warm balmy night. I had been allowed to stay up and we were all sitting in the front porch, when the sound of a nightjar calling, not far off, aroused Hudson.

We followed him silently to the top of the garden, and there in the next field, we hid under some bushes. I was under a gorse bush and had to keep motionless and silent in spite of its prickles.

Then Hudson began calling to the birds, imitating their whirring rattle perfectly. Soon a nightjar answered him, then after a pause Hudson called again, and so it went on, bird and man calling to each other until in the end, the birds—for there were more than one—came to investigate. There was a sudden clap of wings over our heads and a dark shadowy bird whirled away, then another warning clap of wings as another swept over and discovered the impostor. After that it was no good, and we got up, brushed the leaves and prickles off our clothes and walked back, delighted by our sudden contact with the nightjars.

There were glow-worms that night in the grass, and it was then that I told Hudson that I had seen a phosphorescent light like a chain of green beads and, on lighting a match, had found a centipede. Once again my observation was confirmed and I won praise.

Another visitor who came about that time was a short, thickset man of great energy and determined character—Hilaire Belloc. During his visits, he seldom listened to anything my parents said and never stopped talking; he sat up late drinking wine and talking to my father and then got up much too early the next morning. But he not only had energy within himself; he imparted it to all of us, and for a short time after his visit, the defeatist atmosphere that my father's philosophy imparted to me was blown away.

Nothing in the world could be more poisonous to a boy than that philosophy. For Edward usually spoke as though he believed that the finest talents were never recognized; the most sensitive and charming people were ruined and oppressed by the coarse and brutal; that the survival of the fittest meant that ruthlessness, brutality, ugliness and stupidity triumphed and exterminated the beautiful, the sensitive and the gifted. And I was, of course, axiomatically to regard myself as one of the doomed minority. This philosophy, which might have had some truth in it had it been propounded by the Last of the Mohicans, was grotesque nonsense. But I did not realize what nonsense it was until I was nearly twenty, when one day I said to myself:

For hundreds of thousand of years the weakly and the stupid have died; the ugly girls have gone unwed and the beautiful ones been chosen for the mothers of the race by the strongest and most intelligent men. I and everyone else in the world are the inheritors of the successful: why should I fail now when the blood of the winners in life's race runs through my veins? I will not identify myself with a dinosaur.

The memory of Hilaire Belloc's self-confidence faded away; a more lasting memorial of one of his visits was a huge red-and-yellow casserole which he sent to my mother for making *bœuf en daube*.

A far more frequent visitor, and one more congenial to Constance, was a bald serious man of about Edward's age who was to become for many years a close friend of both my parents. He wrote to Constance,[2] in the first instance, because he admired the works of Turgenev, which he had read in her

---

[2] Constance Garnett, the author's mother, translator of Turgenev, Tolstoy and Dostoevsky.

translations, and had himself literary ambitions. Indeed, he had already published a novel and a volume of verses under the *Nom de plume* of John Sinjohn. He was John Galsworthy, and my parents invited him down to the Cearne and at once adopted the position of his literary mentors.

On his first visit he arrived at the same time as a cat with a kitten. Before departing on holiday with their family, some neighbours, knowing us as cat-lovers, brought us their half-wild cat which had newly kittened. Two days later I found our palsied dog, Puppsie, bouncing in on the cat and the kitten in the big room. I rushed forward and grabbed Puppsie by the collar and dragging him away when the cat sprang at me and, missing my eye, tore my eyebrow asunder. In spite of the pain and one eye being full of blood, I remember looking with awe at the mother cat, which had sprung on to the mantelpiece where she remained with arched back and rigid tail, a spitting fury.

The incident had unhinged her, and she subsequently attacked everyone who entered the room. Jack Galsworthy was scratched, though not so severely as I. At last she was trapped in a basket, and Jack and Constance carried the yowling animal and its kitten back to their home, where they liberated them in a woodshed, leaving enough provisions for a few days.

Most of the people I had hitherto known would have been flustered or would have reacted in some way to the savage fury of the maddened animal yowling horribly and tearing at the wicker-basket. Galsworthy did not react; he remained calmly detached. The cat might have been gently purring for all the emotional response it evoked from him. On one of his early visits the miscreant Puppsie dug up and was dragging a bullock's head into the house, which had been bought many weeks before with some intention of making soup, or feeding the dogs, but which had been buried because bluebottles had laid their eggs on it. These had now reached their greatest development, and maggots were falling from it in legions when my mother and Galsworthy intercepted Puppsie with it in the hall. The literary aspirant did not turn a hair, though the stench would have overpowered most people. He calmly fetched a shovel and a wheelbarrow, conveyed the horrible object to the bottom of the garden, dug a large hole, buried it and then returned to wash his hands carefully and dust his knees with a handkerchief scented with a few drops of eau de cologne.

My chief interest in Galsworthy was that he had stalked deer with a Red Indian guide. He was kind and generous to me, and I rewarded him with the honourable title of Running Elk.

At this stage of his life he was in violent revolt against the Forsyte traditions, and my parents influenced him considerably and not only with literary advice. It was from Edward that Galsworthy drew Bosinney in *The Man of Property*—which gives a certain piquancy to the violent discussion, published in their correspondence, in which Edward assailed Jack for not understanding Bosinney's character, and Bosinney's creator defended himself as best as he might. The reason for Galsworthy's revolt against the Forsyte traditions of his family was that he was in love with Irene (Ada), who was married to his cousin.

For several years he was deeply unhappy, and all his best work was written at this time. Finally, after his father's death, Jack and Ada resolved to take the decisive step; she left her husband and went to the man she loved. From that moment Galsworthy was finished as a serious writer. He was happy; he soon became successful and influential, and his natural goodness, his serious desire to assist all the deserving causes near to his heart, ruined his talent. Ada was a sensitive and beautiful woman, with dark hair turning grey and brown eyes, and there was something about her that made me recall bumble bees seen among the velvety petals of dark wallflowers.

Later on, when I was about fifteen, I remember going with Constance and the Galsworthys to a concert. On taking our seats, Ada unpinned her toque and skewered it on to the back of the stall in front with a steel hatpin. Shortly afterwards a gentleman was shown to the seat in front of her. He sat down and leant heavily back in it. There was a violent exclamation and he jumped up. Ada was overwhelmed with concern, which was not dispelled by the gentleman exclaiming: 'Madam, you might have caused my instant death!' and his departing in search of a doctor. During the interval he returned and took his seat in a gingerly manner and, when the concert was over, informed Jack that the doctor thought no vital organ had been touched. I thought the whole incident was extremely comic, and the deep and anxious concern of Jack and Ada added to my amusement, so that I found a good deal of difficulty in suppressing my merriment. My mother also grew very flushed in the face for the same reason. I don't think any of us was able to devote full attention to the music.

I met H.G. Wells for the first time when I was about thirteen or fourteen, when he was brought over two or three times to the Cearne by Sydney Olivier and his daughters. I can see him now as I first saw him, a small figure, bouncing along like a rubber ball between the tall figures of Edward and Sydney, each a head taller than he was, like a boy walking between two men, and all three walking in quite different ways. Edward walked in a long, casual, lurching stride, H.G. Wells positively bounced with ill-suppressed energy, and Olivier strode with aloof dignity, apparently unaware of his companions, to whom he was really listening attentively.

On another occasion, Wells was brought by the Oliviers' girls alone, and I walked back with them. H.G's liveliness and activity dominated all of us, and I remember his instant response to Brynhild's sparkling eyes and flashing smile. But any attraction they felt for each other was suppressed and its expression averted when he played a violent game of rounders after tea.

Wells was, at the time I first saw him, an active figure in the Fabian Society and, when a clash arose between him and the Webbs, my father joined the Society purely in order to vote for Wells and Wells's supporters, when they put up for the Executive Committee. A month later, when Wells had been defeated, Edward resigned.

Constance was quite indignant with him over this: he was not a socialist and had no business to pretend to be one merely in order to take part in a fight; but Edward only laughed and left his defence to Maitland, who supported Wells.

H.G. had already caused uneasiness among the conventional owing to his lack of respect for the taboos attaching to sexual desires and, at one moment Lady Olivier forbade her daughters to read *The Sea Lady*. I remember that Brynhild and Margery poured out their indignation to Edward.

But a little while after I had left University College School, Wells moved to church Row, Hampstead, and the scandal of Annu Veronica broke. The row was prodigious and a considerable portion of it reached my ears. In his *Experiment in Autobiography*, Wells explains that, like many of his characters, the heroine of *Ann Veronica* was suggested by an actual young woman, who is represented as taking the initiative in sexual relations with a demonstrator in Zoology, a typically Wellsian hero. My memory is that the outraged parents of this young woman attempted to destroy Wells, who became the target for a fantastic social persecution. He was turned out of his club—the Savile—and he and his wife were cut and boycotted, in particular by many socialists who were afraid he would fasten the label of Free Love for ever to the movement.

Shaw, unlike the Webbs, who hated Wells, was one of the few of the leading Fabians to behave with common sense; he urged all concerned to hush up the scandal. But it was too late.

Olivier, though remaining most friendly with Wells, wrote to him at this time a moderate and sensible letter, saying he would not like Wells to be seen in public in the company of his daughters. This letter was the cause of a strange scene at the very height of the scandal. I went one day with Brynhild to an exhibition of paintings in Bond Street. After we had been there some time, she suddenly caught sight of Wells, who was hiding from us behind some pictures on a stand running down the middle of the room. Brynhild called out to him in her clear voice and Wells turned and fled like a rabbit. But he took refuge in a cul-de-sac, and Brynhild and I followed and ran him to earth. Her cheeks were scarlet as she held out her hand and her eyes flashed more than ever as she said:

'I won't let you cut me, Mr Wells, so don't ever dare to try to do so again.'

I don't think I ever saw her look lovelier than she did at that moment. She held Wells in talk for five minutes and forced him to look at some of the pictures with us. I could see Wells put into some of the games he made us play. There was rampageous bumping around a table and knocking over of chairs when I had expected to sit around, on my good behavior, listening to highbrow conversation. And then I was dragged into a nursery where a little war was in progress and saw H.G. Wells, in a whirlwind of tactical enthusiasm, ousting his small sons Frank and Gyp from the peaceful enjoyment of their toy soldiers.

I don't think Wells took much notice of me then: but a year or two later, meeting me by the Hampstead Fire Station, opposite the Tube, he said: 'You are following exactly in my footsteps and I suppose later on you'll throw up biology to write novels.' It turned out that he was right in that prophecy as in so many others.

–From *The Golden Echo*

THE LAST LESSON

Alphonse Daudet

I started for school very late that morning and was in great dread of a scolding, especially because M. Hamel had said that he would question us on participles, and I did not know the first word about them. For a moment I thought of running away and spending the day out of doors. It was so warm, so bright! The birds were chirping at the edge of the woods; and in the open field, back of the saw-mill, the Prussian soldiers were drilling. It was all much more tempting than the rule for participles, but I had the strength to resist, and hurried off to school.

When I passed the town hall there was a crowd in front of the bulletin board. For the last two years all our bad news had come from there—the lost battles, ties, the draft, the orders of the commanding officer—and I thought to myself, without stopping:

'What can be the matter now?'

Then, as I hurried by as fast as I could go, the blacksmith, Wachter, who was there, with his apprentice, reading the bulletin, called after me:

'Don't go so fast, bub; you'll get to your school in plenty of time!'

I thought he was making fun of me, and I reached M. Hamel's little garden all out of breath.

Usually, when school began, there was a great bustle, which could be heard out in the street, the opening and closing of desks, lessons repeated in unison, very loud, with our hands over our ears to understand better, and the teacher's great ruler rapping on the table. But now it was all so still! I had counted on the commotion to get to my desk without being seen; but, of course, that day everything had to be as quiet as Sunday morning. Through the window I saw my classmates, already in their places, and M. Hamel walking up and down with his terrible iron ruler under his arm. I had to open the door and go in before everybody. You can imagine how I blushed and how frightened I was.

But nothing happened. M. Hamel saw me and said very kindly:

'Go to your place quickly, little Franz. We were beginning without you.'

I jumped over the bench and sat down at my desk. Not till then, when I had got a little over my fright, did I see that our teacher had on his beautiful green coat, his frilled shirt, and the little black silk cap, all embroidered, that he never wore except on inspection and prize days. Besides, the whole school seemed so strange and solemn. But the thing that surprised me most was to see, on the back benches that were always empty, the village people were sitting quietly like ourselves; old Hauser, with his three-cornered hat, the former mayor, the former postmaster, and several others besides. Everybody looked sad; and Hauser had brought an old primer, thumbed at the edges, and he held it open on his knees with his great spectacles lying across the pages.

While I was wondering about it all, M. Hamel mounted his chair, and, in the same grave and gentle tone which he had used to me, said:

'My children, this is the last lesson I shall give you. The order has come from Berlin to teach only German in the schools of Alsace and Lorraine. The new master will come tomorrow. This is your last French lesson. I want you to be very attentive.'

What a thunderclap these words were to me!

Oh, the wretches; that was what they had put up at the town hall!

My last French lesson! Why, I hardly knew how to write! I should never learn any more! I must stop there, then! Oh, how sorry I was for not learning my lessons, for seeking birds' eggs, or going sliding on the Saar! My books, that had seemed such a nuisance a while ago, so heavy to carry, my grammar, and my history of the saints, were old friends now that I couldn't give up. And M. Hamel, too; the idea that he was going away, that I should never see him again, made me forget all about his ruler and how cranky he was.

Poor man! It was in honour of this last lesson that he had put on his fine Sunday-clothes, and now I understood why the old men of the village were sitting there in the back of the room. It was because they were sorry, too, that they had not gone to school more. It was their way of thanking our master for his forty years of faithful service and of showing their respect for the country that was theirs no more.

While I was thinking of all this, I heard my name called. It was my turn to recite. What would I not have given to be able to say that dreadful rule for the participle all through, very loud and clear, and without one mistake? But I got mixed up on the first words and stood there, holding on to my desk, my heart beating, and not daring to look up. I heard M. Hamel say to me:

'I won't scold you, little Franz; you must feel bad enough. See how it is! Every day we have said to ourselves: "Bah! I've plenty of time. I'll learn it tomorrow." And now you see where we've come out. Ah, that's the great trouble with Alsace; she puts off learning till tomorrow. Now those fellows out there will have the right to say to you: "How is it; you pretend to be Frenchmen, and yet you can neither speak nor write your own language?" But you are not the worst, poor little Franz. We've all a great deal to reproach ourselves with.

'Your parents were not anxious enough to have you learn. They preferred to put you to work on a farm or at the mills, so as to have a little more money. And I? I've been to blame also. Have I not often sent you to water my flowers instead of asking you to learn your lessons? And when I wanted to go fishing, did I not just give you a holiday?'

Then, from one thing to another, M. Hamel went on to talk of the French language, saying that it was the most beautiful language in the world—the clearest, the most logical; that we must guard it among us and never forget it, because when people are enslaved, as long as they hold fast to their language it is as if they had the key to their prison. Then he opened a grammar book and read our lesson. I was amazed to see how well I understood it. All he said seemed so easy, so easy! I think, too, that I had never listened so carefully, and that he had never explained everything with so much patience. It seemed almost as if the poor man wanted to give us all he knew before going away, and to put it all into our heads at one stroke.

After the grammar, we had a lesson in writing. That day M. Hamel had new copies for us, written in a beautiful round hand: France, Alsace, France, Alsace. They looked like little flags floating everywhere in the schoolroom, hung from the rod at the top of our desks. You ought to have seen how every one set to work, and how quiet it was! The only sound was the scratching of the pens over the paper. Once some beetles flew in; but nobody paid any attention to them, not even the littlest ones, who worked right on tracing their fish-hooks, as if that was French, too. On the roof the pigeons cooed very low, and I thought to myself:

'Will they make them sing in German, even the pigeons?'

Whenever I looked up from my writing I saw M. Hamel sitting motionless in his chair and gazing first at one thing, then at another, as if he wanted to fix in his mind just how everything looked in that little schoolroom. Fancy! For forty years he had been there in the same place, with his garden outside the window and his class in front of him, just like that. Only the desks and benches had been worn smooth; the walnut trees in the garden were taller, and the hop-vine that he had planted himself twined about the windows to the roof. How it must have broken his heart to leave it all, poor man; to hear his sister moving about in the room above, packing their trunks! For they must leave the country next day.

But he had the courage to hear every lesson to the very last. After the writing, we had a lesson in history, and then the babies chanted their ba, be, bi, bo, bu. Down there at the back of the room old Hauser had put on his spectacles and, holding his primer in both hands, spelled the letters with them. You could see that he, too, was crying; his voice trembled with emotion, and it was so funny to hear him that we all wanted to laugh and cry. Ah, how well I remember it, that last lesson!

All at once the church-clock struck twelve. Then the Angelus. At the same moment the trumpets of the Prussians, returning from drill, sounded under our windows. M. Hamel stood up, very pale, in his chair. I never saw him look so tall.

'My friends,' said he, 'I—I—' But something choked him. He could not go on.

Then he turned to the blackboard, took a piece of chalk, and, bearing on with all his might, he wrote as large as he could: 'Vive La France!'

Then he stopped and leaned his head against the wall, and, without a word, he made a gesture to us with his hand:

'School is dismissed—you may go.'